Dear Santa

I've been a good boy ALL year. Almost. Mommy said I could rite and tell you my biggest wish. More than anything in the *whole* world I want XXXOOOXXX.

Love Toby

What did Toby want?

Why did Santa think bringing Jeanne and Ron together might be the answer?

Dear Reader,

Happy Holidays! Once again, this joyful time of year is upon us, filled with merriment and good wishes toward all.

But we all know what a frantic time this can be. So may we humbly suggest that in between the shopping, the parties and the decorating, what better way to enjoy the season than by kicking off your heels, and relaxing for a few good hours with Love & Laughter. A little vacation away with Christmas-themed books. (In these stories, let our characters bake the cookies and think of that last-minute present.)

The always scintillating and sensational Tiffany White has created *The 6' 1" Grinch,* a delightful story of a man who hates Christmas! And talented and terrific Leandra Logan spins a warmhearted tale of a little boy's Christmas wish in *Santa and Son*. (Only one guess as to what Toby wants.)

Wishing you a season filled with love—and laughter.

Malle Vallik
Associate Senior Editor

SANTA AND SON

Leandra Logan

Harlequin Books

TORONTO • NEW YORK • LONDON
AMSTERDAM • PARIS • SYDNEY • HAMBURG
STOCKHOLM • ATHENS • TOKYO • MILAN
MADRID • WARSAW • BUDAPEST • AUCKLAND

ISBN 0-373-44010-3

SANTA AND SON

This edition published by arrangement with Harlequin Books S.A.

Printed in U.S.A.

Leandra loves the holiday season, shopping for family and friends. Never one to pass up the chance to browse through a toy store, she's seen her share of Santas on duty, watched them in action from afar. Her husband has yet to endorse the idea of her posing on St. Nick's lap for a photo, but hope springs eternal for next year!

Leandra's next book, a Temptation novel featuring the ever-popular groom-on-the-run theme, will be available in the spring.

Books by Leandra Logan

HARLEQUIN TEMPTATION

472—JOYRIDE
491—HER FAVORITE HUSBAND
519—HAPPY BIRTHDAY, BABY
535—BARGAIN BASEMENT BABY
564—ANGEL BABY
611—HEAVEN-SENT HUSBAND

HARLEQUIN AMERICAN ROMANCE

559—SECRET AGENT DAD
601—THE LAST BRIDESMAID

For Marilu LaVoie

We can still be dangerous
when we want to be!

1

SHE WANTED SANTA and she wanted him bad.

Or so Ron Coleman suspected from the moment the shapely blonde entered Grace Brothers Toys late that wintry Monday afternoon. He had a bird's eye view of the store from the grand North Pole display located at the rear of the center aisle, and had noticed her the minute she'd burst through the sliding-door entrance on a tidal wave of bundled-up shoppers. While others rushed the customer-service area to grab yellow shopping carts and baskets, she broke free of the pack, and moved quickly and with determination toward the center aisle.

The bachelor in him enjoyed watching her. A pale blue parka with a fur-trimmed hood hugged her hourglass torso, and navy stretch pants set her slender legs to advantage. She would've been a welcome elfin addition to Gracie's—as the store was known locally—holiday kingdom. He envisioned her in one of the store's skimpy green-velvet skirts trimmed with white fur, a jaunty tasseled hat in place of her tam, a jolly grin supplanting her frown.

His journalist side, however, seasoned by years of traveling the globe as if it were a routine spin around the park, was concerned about that frown, and her lack of interest in the colorful Christmas gimmickry contrived to catch the eye and urge open the pocketbook. The store's lush brochure featuring Emmett Windom, Minnesota's beloved thespian as this year's Santa Claus, was the most ominous sign of all. By the way the glossy paper was clenched in her gloved hand, Ron was certain her thumb was pressed directly into his grandfather's jugular.

What had his Grandpa Emmett done wrong? Ron wondered. He'd been the store's Santa for two weeks and everything had run as smoothly until now. Ron knew so for a fact. He'd arrived in the Twin Cities shortly after Thanksgiving, and had moved into Emmett's St. Paul high-rise for the holidays to keep an eye on the free-spirited eighty-year-old so his folks could take a worry-free vacation in Arizona. He and his grandfather had bonded like a couple of rowdy boys despite the fifty years between them, and had been having a wonderful time hitting all the best restaurants and theaters during Emmett's off-duty hours.

What bad luck that Ron now happened to be rummaging through the lavish display for Emmett's precious gold pocket watch long after Santa and his entourage of elves were gone for the day. Had the Pole been empty, the Closed sign hanging from the gingerbread-shaped entrance might have been enough to discourage her.

As he dug around the white velvet cushion on the seat of Santa's giant chair, he managed to keep sight of her progress out of the corner of his eye. She was closing in fast. And spoke just as he spotted the timepiece wedged deep behind the cushion.

"Excuse me. Sir?"

The feminine voice was crisp and powerful enough to rise easily above the hum of the crowd and the instrumental version of "Jingle Bells" on the public-address system. Ron straightened and dropped the watch in the pocket of his tweed jacket. He slowly turned to confront her, hoping for a facial flaw—a wart on her chin, perhaps—to detract from her appeal, make this brush-off easy.

As luck would have it, she was even more stunning up close, with cheekbones set startlingly high in a heart-shaped face of the creamiest color and golden hair spilling over her shoulders and the fur ridge of her hood like melted butter.

He was intrigued by the anger behind eyes a shade darker than her jacket, and couldn't help but imagine the explosion, when she did let loose.

Ordinarily he adored such fireworks, lit many a feminine fuse himself to start the sizzle. But this was Emmett's turf, not his! His folks were counting on him to keep the peace, make sure the old guy was safe and sound.

She seemed a little disconcerted by his appraisal. But her words were spiked with annoyance just the same. "Can you tell me who is in charge of Santa Claus?"

"Mrs. Claus?" he quipped.

Her smooth brown brows inched up her soft forehead with traces of suspicion. "You do work here, don't you?"

He glanced down at his sport coat and woolen trousers. He was dressed for the part and could pretend to be a store manager for the cause. With any luck he might even be able to keep this situation from Grace Brothers' true and tyrannical manager, Stanley Bickel. "Santa is in my care," he replied carefully, pleased with his clever tap dance around the truth. "My name is Ron Coleman. And yours is..."

"Jeanne Trent," she said hastily, as though her identity was inconsequential.

"Snowing outside, Ms. Trent?"

"Not yet. I—"

"It's in the forecast I think. You hear anything on the way over?"

Ron's questions were outright manipulation, attempts at distraction. But it was obvious that this beauty couldn't be steered off course. Her dark blue eyes glittered with an unwavering intensity.

"Look, I'm not here to discuss the weather. I have a complaint about your Santa." Her fingers curled into fists, crushing Emmett's brochure with a crackle that made Ron wince. "He's...he's ruined me! And he's going to pay!"

"Shhhh!" Ron's panic rose with her voice. A few shoppers near a shelf of dump trucks turned to survey them. He scrambled down the throne's three steps, past the gumdrop lamp posts, beneath the hanging icicles, and joined her under the gingerbread entrance.

"I will not shush!" she cried, her cheeks aflame.

"Look, Emmett hasn't ruined a woman in ages."

"How can you possibly know that for sure?"

He didn't, of course. The bluff had been automatic. All he knew was that perhaps Emmett wasn't suited for this touchy public-relations job. Playing Santa was just another gig to him. An important one, yes, but a perilous stretch for the salty stage actor who'd never warmed to children outside of his daughter and grandson.

It seemed to Ron that he'd turned around and Emmett had grown old on him. Emmett still behaved like a rogue and his giant ego hadn't diminished any, but this visit Ron saw a frailty and vulnerability in him that hadn't been there before. All in all, how dangerous could one old man be? It took all Ron's courage to pose the all-important question. He cleared his throat, and forced the words to the surface. "Uh, exactly what did he do to you?"

She'd tipped her gaze up to his. "The unthinkable," she said succinctly. "The unforgivable."

Why, the old coot, he thought in stunned surprise. He didn't know whether to ground Grandpa or pat him on the back. How did he do it? Jeanne Trent had to be in her mid-twenties! By all rights Jeanne Trent was more *his* style!

"Are you going to take action or not?" she sputtered.

"Would you mind lowering your voice?" Ron scanned the area for Stanley Bickel. The manager's radar for trouble zoomed in on more shoplifters and merchandise abusers in any given day than his own professional security people did.

"So much for the customer always being right," she fumed, tapping the toe of her black boot like a small jackhammer.

"Well, I'm sure you are right," he said placatingly. "About something. About everything!" He sounded patronizing and ridiculous.

"Oh, you're a typical store employee, all right," she huffed. "Full of empty charm."

Empty charm, eh? Despite the fact that he had no connection to merchandising, her words stung. Emmett wasn't the only one in the family with a huge ego, the only one who could cause some pillage and ruin! He gave her his most captivating smile—The Look. The big gun, the one he pulled out after the most fulfilling kind of lovemaking, the one that had gotten him the most in-depth interviews of his journalism career.

"Now do you really think you're being fair, Jeanne Trent?" he scolded silkily.

"Fair? Me?" Jeanne's voice had risen to a squeak. Where was this conversation headed? On a merry chase going nowhere, common sense told her. He was toying with her, using her complaint as an excuse to flirt—to distract her from her mission.

And distract her he had. She hesitated a moment and studied his gorgeous brown eyes and generous, wolfish mouth. She was a photographer and he certainly was photogenic.

She was also a woman, and it was at that moment that she realized a girl could get in a lot of trouble with a man like Ron Coleman. Knee-knocking, heart-skipping, mattress-dipping trouble.

He was getting places, Ron realized with satisfaction. She wasn't smitten, but she was... interested. If only there was more time to explore this captivating elf. But Bickel was an ever-present threat, as was Emmett himself, currently changing his clothes in the employees' lounge. "I still have no idea what the matter is," he said. "Can't help you till I do."

How sneaky to lay the blame for their verbal detour on her! If the man wasn't a direct descendent of the Grace brothers, he ought to be adopted posthaste. He was a natural who could sell anything—especially himself. She cleared her throat. "My son had a talk with Santa yesterday, and you know what Santa did?"

Ron's eyes grew in confusion. "Hit on you?"

"He promised him everything on his wish list," she lamented as though not hearing him. "Now does that seem right to you?"

"Well—"

"Of course not! Far more tact was in order. I thought these guys went through some kind of training—in evasive tactics, subterfuge, surface platitudes." She paused then. "You mean to say you thought Santa tried to pick me up?"

Ron rubbed his lips, struggling for something clever. "Uh—"

"Why, I wasn't even along," she surged on. "My mother brought Toby." She glared down at the brochure featuring the very old man. "The idea of him hitting on me. The idea that you'd suspect it!"

"Guess I overreacted," Ron admitted resignedly. "A lot of men would be tempted to try to pick you up. I mean, with no wedding ring on your finger..."

Splashes of red appeared on her cheeks as she shook Emmett's brochure. "This guy's old enough to be your grandfather. How could you seriously think that he'd come on to me?"

Because Emmett *was* his grandfather, Ron thought, amused by the irony, and a one-of-a-kind actor character who considered any female old enough to order a martini fair game.

"Furthermore," she continued in a huff, "it's nobody's business why I'm not wearing a wedding ring. I didn't come here to discuss my life with you or anybody else."

Ron groaned inwardly. When had he lost control of this conversation? Why had he deliberately strung her along when he should've gotten rid of her right off?

Because she was just too interesting. Too pretty and fiesty and testy. Too much!

"Look, I think the Better Business Bureau would be interested to learn of a toy store that makes such rash guarantees to encourage sales. It's—it's nothing short of blackmail!"

"Huh?" He couldn't resist touching her arm then. Just a little squeeze on her downy jacket sleeve. "You're jumping to all kinds of inaccurate conclusions. Why, Grace Brothers Toys is not just any store, its known around the world for its unique personality."

"So was John Dillinger," she retorted, "but I wouldn't have trusted him with my son's Christmas happiness."

A frown wedged Ron's brows together. "I happen to know our Santa very well and can absolutely guarantee that he operates with the best intentions."

She waved her glove dismissively, deftly loosening his gentle grip. "So you're willing to admit he may have accidentially slipped up?"

"Yes, of course."

"So what are you going to do about it?"

Damned if he knew. Ron glanced around again to see Stanley Bickel marching up the game aisle, a cross between a watchful sentry and a smug ruler as he inspected his castle. "I'm more than willing to make good here. Meet any promises." His impassioned words bounced back at his face with the sting of a heavy, wet snowball. What if the boy had asked for a four-wheel truck or a trip to Disneyland, or an addition to the house?

Her mouth curled mockingly. "You needn't look so frightened. He is only four years old."

"Oh." He grinned in relief.

"Besides, what I want is free."

Ron gave Bickel another glance. The manager was closer, but had paused to check his reflection in one of the store's many mirrors. He was tugging at the suit coat buttoned over his tubby chest and had produced a comb to adjust his black, slicked-back hair.

He offered her a coaxing smile. "Free, you say?" As if anything in this world was!

"I'm a single parent, and therefore on a tight budget. There will never be a Christmas in my son's young life when he receives everything on his list. If your Santa would be so kind as to retract his promises, admit to making a mistake, I would consider the matter closed."

She was reasonable, lovely, and intelligent. Why did he have to meet her this way, caught up in a tangle of lies? "Your offer sounds more than fair to me." Ron slipped his hand into the lining pocket of his jacket and produced his ever-present leather notepad and pen set. "You can reach me here." He scribbled Emmett's number, and tore the sheet free with a quick snap. "If you don't mind, I'd like to settle this away from the store."

Jeanne put the paper in her small shoulder bag and presented him with one of her business cards. "Seems like a lot of trouble. Dressing up Santa for an extra showing. I could bring Toby back here to—"

"No, no, let's keep this between ourselves." After all, Emmett was bound to find dressing up easier than being strung up. If this leaked out to Bickel the old duffer would be through. "It would undoubtedly disrupt the customer flow," he said, striving for authenticity with some merchandising lingo. "And there is the photographer. We, ah, have an agreement with her about snapping each child who sits upon the jolly man's knee."

"Yes, about that photograph..."

He cringed as she launched into a spiel about how some better lighting, and different angles could improve the shots. Hope that she might perhaps be a forgettable know-it-all began to grow until he glanced at her card to find the slogan Pretty as a Picture printed on the top. She had every right to believe, as a manager, he'd be interested in her professional criticism. And dammit, it made her all the more intriguing.

But enough was enough. As much as he enjoyed her soft husky voice and the way her blue eyes danced, he had no more time to play store. Not only did he have to concern himself with Stanley Bickel, but Emmett as well. He was just emerging from the employee lounge several yards away, easing into his topcoat. A collision between all of them would be a disaster. Jeanne would unload, Bickel would explode, and poor Emmett would be forced to hit the road.

"Jeanne," he began with deliberate silkiness, "perhaps we could talk about all this later on. I have an important meeting to attend—some of my cashiers have been overloading the bags at the checkouts." The moment the excuse popped out, he realized how lame it was. All a real manager would have to do is walk over and tell the clerks not to be so stingy with the bags. Obviously, there was no time for a meeting during this mad rush!

"I see," she said succinctly between small even teeth. "This could really backfire if the press ever got hold of it."

Didn't he know it! He'd be the first in line to write an exposé if there was any reason to believe Gracie's Santa was dishonest! He couldn't help noting that Bickel was now closing in on them. "Look, I have your number."

"And I think I have yours," she returned icily. "Prove me wrong." With that parting gibe she turned on her heel and retreated down the wide center aisle.

"Ah, Ronald!" Emmett lifted his hand in greeting as he approached.

All traces of Santa had vanished. With his cashmere topcoat, his crest of carefully groomed salt-and-pepper hair, Emmett now looked more like a visiting British aristocrat, his favorite image in public.

"Did you manage to find my timepiece, boy?" he asked with a dash of urgency.

Ron withdrew it from his pocket.

"Spendid, splendid." Emmett hooked the gold chain to his belt loop, seemingly unaware that Stanley Bickel had joined them.

"So, Emmett, how did things go today?" Bickel asked solicitously.

"Splendid, splendid." Emmett used this hearty refrain in the store in order to maintain a distant and positive image.

It was common knowledge among Gracie employees that Bickel was just looking for some excuse to dump this version of jolly old St. Nick. Bickel had been forced to take on Emmett by Wendell Grace himself, the eldest of the Grace brothers and a theater buff who considered Emmett's stage prowess second only to Sir Laurence Olivier's. Bickel fancied himself the real power behind Gracies, and he'd promised the Santa position to a cousin in advance. Apparently the cousin was waiting in the wings, until Bickel could justify the old man's dismissal.

How ironic that Bickel had let Jeanne Trent go without an introduction, Ron thought with grim satisfaction, when she was the answer to his prayers—Emmett's first and only critic on this gig.

"So, Ron," Emmett said, "who was the woman who cornered you under the gingerbread?"

"A friend," Ron replied evenly, picking up his brown leather jacket, draped over a plastic snowdrift.

"Somebody you know from the old days, eh?" Bickel ventured.

Ron shrugged into the thigh-length coat, and concentrated on the buttons to disguise his wry grin. "Your level of intuition never wavers, Stanley."

The prissy man beamed. "Yes, I have a knack for such things. Tough to pull a fast one here in my kingdom."

"I'm sure." With a curt nod, Ron took hold of Emmett's elbow. "C'mon, Pop, I'm starved."

"Won't be having chicken again tonight," Emmett cautioned him as they moved through the crowd. "I want steak, burnt crisp with a juicy pink middle. To blazes with the cholesterol."

"I have to admit that sounds good for a change," Ron admitted. "We just won't tell Mom."

They paused on the sidewalk outside the store for a moment and watched the rush-hour traffic on Snelling Avenue. Dusk had set in and it was snowing lightly. "Let's head for the Countryview," Emmett suggested. "It's close, on County Road B2."

"Sure thing, Pop."

Emmett turned the collar up on his coat and glared at his grandson. "Stop calling me Pop! Here in the midwest it is a soft drink, not a person. And you know that, a Minnesota boy born and bred."

Of course Ron knew. It wouldn't be fun otherwise. He extracted his keys from his jacket pocket, affecting an innocent smile. "Okay, Grandfather, the car's over here to the right."

Together they crossed the snow-packed blacktop. Even though the Santa display had closed, the lot was still jammed with vehicles.

"Remember, son, in the restaurant, it's Emmett. Ron and Emmett, a couple of fellows out for a bite. A couple of unattached males on the hunt."

Ron inserted his key into the driver's door and released both locks on the rented two-door Plymouth. "Isn't working enough distraction for you?"

Emmett winked at him over the snow-dusted hood. "Why, it's a cover, boy, a sham, a way to meet the ladies."

"Sure, Pop. Nothing comes second to your acting career and we both know it."

"Hah! You used the setting for your own gain just now, didn't you? You may have fooled Bickel about that woman being an old friend, but I certainly didn't buy it. There was absolute terror in your eyes. I didn't think even an exciting stranger could scare the hell out of a seasoned gadabout like you!"

The two men eased into the car. Emmett rubbed his hands together gleefully. "I dare you to tell me all the juicy details."

Ron stared grimly out the windshield as he ignited the engine. "I dare you to try and stop me."

EMMETT BELIEVED it was his social standing that got them a fireside table at the Countryview Steakhouse. Ron didn't argue the issue, but figured his ten-dollar tip hadn't hurt. It was worth every penny to see the old man's chest puff with pride and Ron was enjoying the warmth of the flames. Though he traveled the globe for human interest stories, he spent a good deal of his time at his suburban Los Angeles home, where the climate was always tolerable.

Emmett watched him shiver slightly and take a gulp of his Scotch. "Can't believe you're the same kid who used to toboggan in just a sweatshirt and jeans. Now you act like a trembling pup at the first dip to zero."

"The blood thins after years away, Po—Emmett," he corrected. He nodded at the two middle-aged ladies at the next table who'd been eyeing his grandfather and had made little attempt to disguise their interest.

Ron felt like a fool for his mistakes with Jeanne Trent. To her, Emmett was just an old man but she didn't know his grandfather like he did. Emmett's good looks made him ageless and attractive in a most disarming way. Given the opportunity, Ron had no doubt that Emmett could have gotten her into some kind of delicious trouble.

Not that he wasn't a fitter man for the job, Ron told himself. Even now, he couldn't stop thinking about her, replaying their encounter for his own private pleasure. Unfortunately, it was high time he shared her complaint with Emmett. That should put an end to his fanciful dreaming.

Ron downed the last of his drink and signaled for one last round.

Emmett leaned over the linen-covered table. "I was thinking of inviting our charming companions over for a nightcap. What do you say?"

Ron's brown eyes blazed. "No."

Emmett settled back in his chair with a good-natured chuckle. "All right. Guess the three phone numbers I did get today are enough."

"We have to talk about the blonde—"

"There's something really sexy about that Santa costume, Ronny." Emmett interrupted with twinkling eyes. "The ladies must feel kind of naughty slipping old St. Nick a mash note. Maybe you should get a Santa job of your own. I mean as long as you're just sitting around all month."

"I'm not sitting around," his grandson argued hotly. "You know very well that I'm doing the guest holiday column for the Minneapolis *Clarion* while I'm here." He didn't have the heart to add that filling in for his folks as Emmett's guardian was proving to be a job in itself. It was more than driving him around and making sure he didn't slip in the shower. More than ever, Emmett needed an audience, an adoring audience. A lot of the time, Ron was it.

Emmett drained his Scotch as the waitress brought the fresh ones. "All you do is write in that damn diary of yours."

"It's a journal, Pop, and many a nugget of inspiration has jumped out at me from those pages. Besides, I wonder if you realize how coveted those Santa positions are, and how many men would bend over backwards for one—especially at Grace Brothers!"

"Never resorted to bending over backwards for anybody," Emmett said huffily. "It's one reason why men like us choose to make a living in the arts. Makes it easier to slip by the corporate power-mongers cracking their whips over the pathetically prone."

"Well, Stanley Bickel is a monger to look out for."

"Don't I know it!" Emmett shook his gleaming head. "Poor clerks always dancing to his tune. I intend to have a long talk with Wendell and Arnold Grace. They should really take a deeper interest in store policy."

"The Graces have so many business interests, Emmett," Ron pointed out. "They have the pizza-parlor chain and the menswear stores."

"So?"

"So, it appears they prefer to leave things in Bickel's hands. If you want to keep your job, you should stick with your, 'splendid, splendid' smoke screen. He doesn't seem clever enough to see through it."

"You mean I shouldn't complain to the Graces?"

"At least hold off until the new year."

Emmett's eyes hardened over the rim of his glass. "You look deathly pale, like the time you drove your father's golf cart off the dock at Deer Lake."

"Thanks for that reminder," his grandson retorted. "But you're the one sinking like a rock today. Now about that blonde!"

Emmett reared back. "No need to shout."

Ron took a deep breath, then related Jeanne Trent's story. Emmett listened carefully, absorbing each word with a judge's fortitude.

"So you see, Grandfather, if you do value this job, you will have to try a little harder to work within the system," he said in closing. "Agreeing to see the boy in costume seems like a fair compromise, doesn't it? Listen to his list again, rethink your response."

"Sheer poppycock. Impossible poppycock!"

"Why, Emmett, why?"

"Because I am a method actor," the old man returned coldly. "You've known that all your life. The cheesy model of the North Pole may be just so much child's play to you, but it is my home while I am there. Seated on that throne, dressed in red velvet, I *am* Santa Claus. The genuine article." He raised a long shaky finger, his voice gaining momentum. "Just as I was Hamlet at the Ordway, Othello at the Guthrie, Professor Higgins at the Old Log. The stage of the moment is my reality, the footlights my sunshine, the applause—or mash notes in this case—my manna. In short, Santa Claus does not do retractions. I stand by each and every performance."

Ron seethed. "But you promised this kid everything on his list!"

Emmett shook his head in helpless wonder. "Then I must have had the impression that he was to get everything. Nothing to worry about, son."

Ron pounded the table. "You know what I will have to do, don't you? I will have to make good your promises."

Emmett regarded him blandly. "Don't see why."

Ron was upset enough for both of them and couldn't disguise the fact. "Because Jeanne Trent can't afford to do so. If I don't deliver, she'll eventually get to Bickel and he will gladly fire you. You really should do as she asks."

"Santa does not renege!" A deep rumbling sound surged from Emmett's chest as he lunged to his feet. "Not even for a beautiful woman!" His rich baritone bounced off the paneled walls of the cozy pub-style grill. Heads turned toward him, the room stilled. He perused the tables with flashing eyes. "Nay, my good people. As it happens, the woman I discuss with this newsmonger reminds me of a few lines straight out of *Othello*." He took complete control of the room, his regal figure dramatically backlit by the roaring fireplace. His captive audience waited breathlessly, anxious to watch him deliver. And clutching the lapel of his suit coat, deliver he did.

"My story being done,
She gave me for my pains a world of sighs;
She swore, in faith 'twas strange, 'twas passing strange;
'Twas pitiful, 'twas wonderous pitiful."

The diners broke out in applause. Ron was sure he was breaking out in a rash. If he could have folded his six-foot frame underneath the small table, he would have done so.

"YOU SURE it's bedtime?" Toby Trent was asking at that very moment several miles away in his suburban Roseville bedroom.

Jeanne ruffled her son's thatch of thick, blond hair and leaned over his bed to kiss his soft cheek. "I am very, very sure."

"Tuck me real tight, so I'm like a mommy."

"Mummy, Toby." Jeanne made her way around his bed, securing the covers between the mattress and box spring. At one of the bottom corners her fingers touched upon some kind of paper. She pulled it free to find it was a business-size envelope. "What's this?"

"A letter to Santa."

"When did you write it?"

"Today."

"You mean while I was out?"

"Yeah." His eyes were shiny in the lamplight. "Sherry gave me the paper. Okay?"

She recognized it as her business stationery for Picture Perfect. Naturally the baby-sitter wouldn't know where the cheaper stock was. "It's fine, honey."

"Where'd you go, Mummy?" he asked in a teasing voice.

To tangle with a man so sexy he should be pushing love potions rather than roller skates. Even now, hours later,

Jeanne couldn't completely focus on her original mission at Gracie's. Ron Coleman's runaround made her heart skip over and over again.

"Well, Mummy?"

"I'm Mommy," she protested in teasing dismay, sending him into a fit of giggles. She sat down on the mattress, bracing herself for another attempt to outfox this smaller male, the center of her life. "So, you ready to talk about your Christmas presents tonight?"

His lower lip jutted out above his sheet. "No."

"But you told Santa."

"Course I did."

"So I think you should tell me too."

"Nope. It's a big surprise. I told you over and over."

"I wish you'd try and understand that even Santa can't afford everything," she said gently.

"He said I could have everything. He said so."

Jeanne opened her mouth to protest, then closed it again. She was helpless here. She tried hard to be everything to the child, but she had to draw the line at Santa. He was one person she couldn't imitate, replace, or overrule.

"Santa wouldn't lie to a good boy, would he?" he asked hopefully.

"Not on purpose, Tobe."

"I want to mail my letter tomorrow. Need a stamp. You got a stamp?"

"I think you should draw a nice one."

"You got an address? I need an address."

"We'll do that together." She started a little when he took the letter back, and stuffed it under his pillow with a sly look.

"Did, ah, Sherry help you with your list?"

"Nope."

That was too bad. Sherry would have gladly ratted on him, to help the cause. She tried not to show the disappointment she felt. ‘‘So, what story would you like to hear tonight?’’

‘‘None.’’ His lashes fell to his rounded cheeks. ‘‘I gonna dream all about Christmas.’’

Jeanne left the room feeling defeated. To discover what was on Toby’s list would take time; to acquire all the items would take money. With bills and job commitments piling up, she had little of either. As always, she’d faced the holiday season with the best intentions, but for the first time in her life, she was beginning to identify with Scrooge!

2

"WHEN ARE YOU going to put that boy in school?"

Jeanne, seated at the kitchen table the following morning reading the newspaper, glanced up as her sister Angie entered the kitchen. All the Potters, including Jeanne herself, were aggressive and outspoken, and darn proud of it. But Angie Potter-Gilbert, the eldest of the Potter siblings, was all of these things in the extreme.

Just like their leader, their mentor, their mother: Catherine J. Potter.

Jeanne hid a wince behind her raised coffee cup. She especially hated it when Angie played the child-rearing expert. Big sister and her dentist husband, Brad, had no children as yet. Despite the fact that Angie had no practical experience to draw from, she never tired of offering Jeanne unsolicited advice concerning Toby.

Jeanne sighed. She and her younger brother Andrew had learned at a very young age how to deal with Angie: they allowed her to vent like a seasoned district attorney, then put forward a steady and firm defense.

"Toby is four, and too young for kindergarten," she said evenly. "He is enrolled in fall classes and until then, I feel more than capable of meeting his needs here at home."

"Do you know he greeted me at the door like a butler? 'Remove your shoes,'" Angie mimicked in a childlike squeak. "'Do you got a bappointment?'" She pounded the countertop. "Does he know how children are supposed to behave?"

Jeanne couldn't help laughing. "He was only playing a game."

"How can you tell?"

"For starters, I don't have any appointments scheduled until later on."

"Oh, Jeanne!" Angie lamented. "Why should he even know that in the first place?"

"He's trying to be part of the business. The man of the house. And he really is trying to say 'appointment' properly, but he can't quite get his tongue around that big word."

"He is a child who should be at play!" Angie stripped off her ski jacket dripping with lift tickets and draped it over the empty chair, then pushed aside Toby's cereal bowl and juice cup.

Jeanne gave up on the paper. "He doesn't open the door to strangers. Many of my clients have their pictures taken regularly and are good friends. And I always tell him who's expected. It's not like he hangs around the foyer just waiting to greet Jack the Ripper." There was no point in telling Angie that Toby loved to tease his Aunt Angie the most because she was so easy to bait. A boy didn't need nursery school to evolve into a well-balanced, insightful terror!

Angie poured herself a cup of coffee from the carafe on the counter. "Yes, about the way you run your business," she forged on. "You're still charging your clients hobby fees, aren't you, the way you did when David was alive and photography was only a hobby? The Drillmaster and I were discussing it last night and think you should reevaluate your position, strive to widen your profit margin."

Angie and Brad "Drillmaster" Gilbert had a Dellwood mansion and country-club membership thanks to dental fees that gave them a very healthy profit margin. They gleefully admitted to a relationship full of nonstop discussion, which began during the day when Angie, who acted as Brad's hygienist, babbled incessantly over a steady stream of patients, then into the night while they snuggled in their massive king-size bed. Jeanne felt that if they shut up and rolled around on their plush carpet once in a while, they'd have a child of their own to smother in no time flat!

"I intend to raise my rates after the new year," Jeanne honestly reported. "There's something psychological about it. People more readily accept price hikes in January."

Angie approached the table to refill Jeanne's mug and remove the cavity-causing sugar bowl. "Sure, and all your customers will get their holiday photos at a steal."

"At a good rate, sure. But I'm still making a profit. I—" Jeanne broke off with a sigh as Angie sat down across from her, her nostrils flared like a wild filly, intent on a long gallop down a oft-traveled road. "Angie, I wish you wouldn't pick on me right now. I mean, I really, really wish you wouldn't."

Angie gazed directly into the forlorn face so much like her own, then wound down contritely. "You're right, kid, so right to stop me. You put up such a good front, I sometimes forget how fragile you are."

"I don't like that word, Angie. Fragile. It describes the first few months of widowhood. I'm about to clock in my first year of it. Because David died last January, the first Christmas without him comes on the tail end of all the other firsts. Can you understand that? It's like one last blast of pain, just waiting to grip me at the most sentimental time of year."

"Understand?" Angie crowed. "The whole family is acutely aware of the situation. Mom's baked three times her normal cookie quota. Dad's got the surface of the house plastered with light bulbs. And Andrew—" She stopped short, realizing Jeanne would know that their little brother hadn't gone out of his way at all. Andrew was a twenty-year-old college sophomore who boarded at school and always returned home at the last minute, just in time for all the fun, but none of the work. How Jeanne envied him! And enjoyed his company. He was far too self-centered and fun-loving to butt into her affairs.

"Do me a favor and bully the folks into behaving like the boisterous, egotistical monsters we Potters have always been at Christmas," Jeanne pleaded, reaching across the table to squeeze her sister's hand.

"Don't know if even I can force cheer," she said doubtfully.

"Start with the Drillmaster," Jeanne suggested brightly.

"My husband's not an insane Potter," Angie objected. She took pride in the fact that she'd married a level-headed man with ties to the governor and other sober authority figures.

"Still, he's too solicitous," Jeanne insisted. "Denting my mashed potatoes at Thanksgiving was unnecessary. David looked out for me, but not even he did that."

Angie's voice rose defensively. "Brad just wanted to dent those spuds properly to dam the gravy. He can't stand not perfecting any kind of cavity within reach."

"Dam's a bad word," Toby peeped, peering in from the living-room doorway with huge shiny hazel eyes.

"Not the kind of dam that holds gravy," Angie hastily corrected. "Gravy dams are perfectly fine."

"Okay." With a grin, he vanished.

Angie's forehead puckered as she regarded her sister again. "I'll help you with the folks, if you enroll Toby in one organized activity this spring. The county sponsors all sorts of things—swimming, tumbling, painting. That kid should be needling his peers."

"Well..."

"Stop cringing. You're overprotective. Your son will walk out the door and return unscathed, over and over again." Her voice grew soft as Jeanne's eyes grew moist. "It's a reasonable assumption made by millions of parents each and every day."

"Hold that pose for a minute!" Jeanne ordered, then studied her dumbfounded sister. "You remind me of somebody important. But who? Who?"

Angie did respect Jeanne's eye for imagery. She gave her tide of blond hair a pat, her eyes dancing anxiously. "Loni Anderson? You know I went to her old hairdresser last week for this trim."

Jeanne tipped her head pensively one way, then the other. "No, it's not the hair. It's something about the tone." Her eyes grew dramatically sinister. "Your whiny, demanding tone."

Angie clapped her hands to her cheeks. "Not her! Not Mother!"

Jeanne snapped her fingers. "How shrewd of you to figure it out. Catherine J. Potter uses that annoying voice when things aren't going her way."

"Stop! Stop! I beg you!" Angie became a Potter girl again, completely silly for a brief moment, giggling in a way the Drillmaster himself wouldn't even recognize.

"You stop making reasonable assumptions for me and I'll back off," Jeanne promised.

"Just listen to me on this one issue," Angie pleaded, struggling to recover. "If you want to survive the holidays, at least give the appearance of a budding social life, for both you and Toby. The scales will be out, ready to measure your progress. I have the feeling that if you're not happy, Mother is going to make you happy."

Jeanne lifted her chin in pride. "I'm taking small steps outward that don't have to be faked. I've been appreciating the opposite sex again. In subtle ways."

"Subtle? You mean squeezing mushy off-season cantaloupes at the grocery store with a silent, come-hither look?"

"No, I've graduated from the frozen-food section where I made real conversation. A scintillating debate over brands of chicken potpies and beef pita pockets."

"You never buy that stuff!"

"I know, but that didn't stop me from giving my opinion." Jeanne batted her eyes and puckered her lips.

Angie was openly impressed. "Way to go, flirty babe!"

"Yeah, the poor lamb listened with guileless faith, and bought what I told him to." She gave her head a hair rippling toss. "Oh, the dizzying feel of power."

Angie leaned forward eagerly. "Did he ask for your phone number? Have you seen him again?"

"Heck, no! It was just sort of an experiment. He was no one I'd care to catch under the mistletoe. He was a little pudgy and wore track shoes with rundown heels."

"Oh, sure, destroy the scene for me. I was envisioning 'The Young and the Restless' there for a minute."

"I wish." Jeanne braced her elbow on the tabletop and set her chin in her hand. "I do see what you mean though, about my holiday image. Everybody would relax if they thought I was involved."

"Even a commercial picture from a new wallet would ease the tension."

"What!" Jeanne sat up ramrod stiff, truly affronted for the first time.

"You know, something to flash and slip back into your purse before anybody realized it was a snap of Don Johnson in his salad days."

"I'm not that desperate," Jeanne said emphatically. "Don't you think as a professional photographer I can come up with a finer phony photo than that!"

"Gee, sis," Angie teased, "I apologize for underestimating your social skills."

As Jeanne searched for a scathing comeback, the doorbell rang. "Don't move," she said, bouncing out of her chair. "I'm not through with you yet!"

Toby collided with her in the hallway. "It's a real live stranger!" he reported. "So I just runned away!"

"Good boy." Jeanne ruffled his hair.

She returned to the kitchen moments later to find Angie straightening the cereal boxes in her cupboard. Angie flinched, expecting the usual protest about her compulsive cleaning, but Jeanne barely looked at her. She smacked a red-and-green-striped envelope on the countertop. "That was a messenger."

"Good news, I hope."

"Hah! He thinks he can buy me off with three hundred bucks!"

"Who he?"

"Him!" Jeanne seethed. "Can you imagine the nerve?"

"I can't even imagine *him,*" Angie blurted out in wonder. "Though I'd like to." Brimming with curiosity, Angie grabbed the envelope and peered inside. "A gift certificate for Gracie's. Do you realize most people would kill for this?"

Jeanne jammed a hand on her hip, her mind full of questions. A good deed gone bad? A bad boy doing good? A bad boy paying off?

"What's this Post-it Note mean? 'All the best, Santa.'"

Jeanne snatched it away from her. "Well, he was more like son of Santa, really—age-wise, I mean."

"Who!"

"A guy named Ron Coleman."

"The famous journalist?"

"No, the infamous toy-store superjock."

"Guess there must be two," Angie mumbled. "Never mind, go on."

"Remember, after Sunday dinner how Mom was set to take Toby to Grace Brothers?"

"Yeah, I heard firsthand from her what happened," Angie admitted. "So this is connected to that?"

"Of course. Didn't either one of you think I was going to handle it?"

Angie stroked her sister's flaxen hair. "Simmer down. All Mom said was that you forbade her to go back to fix St.

Nick's hash. I understand full well that you couldn't turn her loose over there, with her temper."

"Exactly! We don't call her Cat for nothing." Jeanne explained the entire situation to her sister.

"It appears that you've done fine," Angie concluded. "So, it's over."

"But I didn't want this kind of payoff. I want Santa himself," Jeanne objected in a whisper, keeping her eye on the doorway for any sign of her inquisitive son. "I wanted him to backpedal on the promises."

"Ninety-nine percent of all Twin Citians would settle for the certificate," Angie declared with confidence.

Jeanne hated the way Angie made up statistics to suit her own viewpoint. "Maybe so, but I feel I've been giving in and making do ever since David died."

"What a dumb cause to start with."

Jeanne caught her sister's gaze and held it. Their blue eyes locked for a long moment. "Would you like to guarantee Toby everything he wants for Christmas, Ange?"

Angie's mouth sagged open. "I... guess it depends upon what he wants."

"He's keeping that a secret."

"Oh." The know-it-all sister was stumped. She took her ski jacket off the back of the chair, and shrugged into it.

Jeanne's voice was husky when she continued. "I figure we're at a crossroads. If he's disappointed this year, after losing David, he may grow up never believing in the spirit of Christmas again."

Angie gulped, thought hard, then said with a resurgence of confidence, "I see what you mean, but surely you can force an answer out of him."

"I've tried. And failed!"

Angie regarded her awe. "I can't believe it's you, sometimes."

Jeanne's pretty face went blank. "What do you mean?"

"The way you've stopped dreaming like a Potter, Sis. The way you fully expect a shadow of disappointment to cross your path at every other turn. Since when is failure even part of our family's vocabulary?"

"It's tougher when you're spinning dreams all by yourself," Jeanne said patiently, but firmly. "I schemed way too big once, and lost the whole jackpot."

"There are other gambles out there, Jeanne. The biggest loss of all would be to stop trying." Angie zipped her jacket. "It's about time I went to the office. Big root canal ahead."

"Oh, sure, get along, you impetuous Potter!" Jeanne tapped the edge of the envelope on her palm. "I just can't believe this," she murmured. "He seemed so anxious to please me."

"Really?" Angie gave her a quick hug, hope springing anew in her features. "Is this Ron Coleman attractive?"

"Extremely so. Tall, muscular frame. Dark brown eyes, large mouth full of teeth you'd be proud to floss. So what's it to ya?"

"So I was just going to suggest you snap his picture for your wallet," Angie said sweetly, wiggling her fingers. "'Bye."

"Don't tell Mom a darn thing about this, Ange. Not a darn thing!"

"A LADY ON THE LINE for you, Ron." A regal Emmett, bedecked in an emerald robe and black hard-soled slippers, held the phone out to his grandson later that same morning, his palm covering the mouthpiece. Ron, who had just finished showering and was wrapped in a towel, held out a wet hand for the receiver.

"Recognize the voice, Pop?"

Emmett's lips thinned. "No."

"Big help," his grandson mouthed as he moved closer.

Emmett's gaze traveled over Ron's lean, damp body with a measure of scorn. "She is most assuredly a lady, however, and you are in no condition to speak to a lady."

Ron nodded curtly, dropped the towel, then took the receiver. "Hello," he said with a hint of laughter in his voice.

"This is Jeanne Trent."

"Oh!" Suddenly Ron felt uncomfortable with his nudity. He made a grab for the towel, but Emmett was a step ahead, already in the process of scooping it up. Ron, tethered by the phone cord, had no choice but to allow his grandfather his little game.

"Got your certificate," she went on, oblivious to everything but her own frustration.

"Hope it's enough. If not—"

"I thought you understood me yesterday. I want Santa himself."

"But the money's better," Ron protested, pacing round like a bronzed warrior with an arrow piercing his hide. Adding insult to injury, Emmett was listening from a safe distance, more than happy to be the audience for a change.

"No, the money isn't better. You get Santa over to my house, ready to make a retraction, or I'll go above your head. There must be somebody in the Grace empire who can overrule you!"

Ron was horrified. This would crush the duffer for sure! "No, wait!"

"I happen to know Santa's in the store from one to five every day of the week," she went on vigorously, pouncing on his distress like a cunning lioness. "If I don't see him before tomorrow, I'll head straight for the North Pole!"

"But I can't. A retraction's—" He broke off as a dial tone buzzed in his ear. He whirled on Emmett. "It seems our late-night trip back to the store for that gift certificate backfired. She still wants you and only you."

"A lady of discrimination and breeding," Emmett surmised.

Ron stomped up and snatched the towel off Emmett's arm. "I have to go out for a while."

"So close to curtain time?" Emmett glanced at the wall clock with a worried look.

"I'll be back in plenty of time to take you to the store." Ron turned slowly, a crafty smile on his face. "Better yet, why not ride along with me now?"

Emmett stroked his jaw. "Well, your sudden engagement does sound intriguing, but I have some things around here that need doing."

"You're just going to stand idly by and let me do your dirty work for you, aren't you?"

Emmett straightened indignantly and grasped the lapels of his robe. "How sharper than a serpent's tooth it is to have a thankless child."

Ron imitated his grandfather's stance, down to clutching an invisible lapel. "Thou shouldst be concerned with this pesky mother, after thy job, thy scrawny neck."

"I swear you could make it on the stage if you wanted to," Emmett marveled as he relaxed his pose. "Your dramatic flair skipped a generation, you know. Lord knows I love your mother, but Bernice is too mature for our extravagant ways."

"As Jeanne Trent seems to be. That kind always follows through."

"Yes, her sort make wonderful wives and daughters." Emmett lifted his sloped shoulders in resignation. "I suppose somebody has to run the shop for us lads."

Ron pressed a hand to his damp and hairy chest. "Please make the retraction, Grandfather. For me, as my Christmas gift."

The old man clutched his lapels harder, his gnarled knuckles whitening. "If I were to do so, I would be a liar to the nth degree. I have spoken what I know to be the truth to all the children and will not give in to a skittish mother who doesn't have enough faith, no matter how pretty she may be." He raised a brow and his voice. "Ah, but that kind does things to a man. Despite the issues, the heart skips with delight."

Ron's brown eyes grew larger. "She's way too young for you."

"Oh, yes, just by a margin." He smiled broadly. "It's your ticker that's up for grabs this round."

"Well, enjoy the show." Ron heaved a beleaguered sigh, and headed back for the bathroom to shave.

"MOMMY! It's a stranger again!"

Jeanne turned away from the tripod holding her best 35mm camera as Toby burst through the door of her in-house studio. "A stranger you know?" she asked, thinking of Santa.

"No way. It's a real stranger!"

"Excuse me a moment, Agnes." Jeanne nodded to her client, and went in pursuit of her son, already on the run again. To her chagrin, she found Ron on her doorstep.

"Oh," she greeted flatly. "It's you." She turned to her son, panting at her side like a frisky, inquisitive puppy. "Toby, go tell Agnes to take five."

"Gotcha." With two thumbs up Toby scooted off.

Ron was primed to press his palm against the door if she tried to close it, but she fooled him by easing out onto the step beside him. He flinched beneath her cold scrutiny. "You do awful things to a guy's ego, you know that?"

She surveyed him, and was aware of mixed emotions. He was so appealing, dressed in indigo jeans, a midlength leather jacket that fit to his broad shoulders and lean hips with tailored perfection. He had a stricken expression that he was attempting to realign into a bland mask of indifference. Was he worked up about Santa or her, or both? "Well, you got here fast enough," she said, saying the only thing she could think of.

He bared his teeth in a cynical smile. "Thank you very much." Emmett's Como Avenue high rise was only ten minutes west of her Roseville home. For all he knew, she and the old man might even shop at the same strip mall on Lexington.

She folded her arms across her chest as the cold air seeped into her royal-blue sweat clothes. "So where is he, Mr.—"

"Please, call me Ron."

She eyed him warily. "Where's the man in red, Ron?"

"You wear blue a lot, don't you?" He ran an appreciative eye over her shivering form.

"Red, Ron, red! Where's Santa?"

He smiled faintly. "It suits you."

"What suits me?"

"Blue. Except around the lips. Aren't you freezing?"

Her mind raced to keep up with him. "Yes, but I have a very nosy little boy with excellent hearing."

"Well, the only gentlemanly thing to do is admit that the man in red isn't coming."

"But why?" Her voice rose shrilly.

"He flat out refuses," Ron reported, watching her dance from one sneaker to another on the cramped stoop.

"But you said you were in charge of him!"

"I said he was in my care," he corrected mildly. "Please, let me in. We really have to talk."

"Give me one reason why I shouldn't march right down to that palace of toys and have you fired. Give me one good reason!"

He lifted his hands in a helpless gesture. "Because I don't work there?"

Her mouth sagged. "Huh?"

"It's true. I'm sorry."

She squealed in despair. "After all I've been through, I won't even have the pleasure of making you squirm?"

"On the contrary." He reached over her and turned the doorknob. "By all means, give it to me good."

3

"HEY, DO I KNOW you?"

Ron was standing in the center of the Trent living room, removing his jacket when he heard the voice behind him. He swiveled round to find a small boy standing in the doorway, dressed in a green sweatshirt and blue jeans. "No, you don't know me." Ron tried to keep up a merry front, but he didn't appreciate being parked in here, although Jeanne had seemed contrite as she explained that there was a client in her studio and she was in the midst of a photo shoot.

"Do you know me?" the child asked intently, sidling closer.

"Nope." They studied each other for a long moment. Ron noted that the child greatly resembled his mother. He had her fair, Nordic features, and high, full cheeks.

"I'm Toby."

Ron draped his jacket on an arm of the sofa and sat down on the center cushion. "I'm Ron."

"You Mommy's friend?"

Ron pressed his hands between his knees. "I want to be."

"Mommy's friends play with me." His eyes sparkled, full of hope and mischief.

"Well, I'm here for a talk—" Ron started as Toby tossed a purple foam rubber ball into his lap. He promptly tossed it back to the boy. "I really don't have time for catch."

"Do so." Toby tossed the ball to Ron.

"I don't, Toby. Really."

Toby turned his back for a second, then spun around with a small vinyl glove on his left hand. When Ron tossed the ball back again, Toby made an unnecessary dive to grab it. "Line drive!" he shouted, reaching out as though he was making a tremendous save. He danced around on the tips of his tennis shoes. "Out on first. Crowd goes wild!"

Ron laughed. "Pretty good. So, you a Minnesota Twin in training?"

"Yup." With that the boy raced out of the living room.

With long-limbed restlessness, Ron rose from the mauve sateen sofa, and took a good look at his surroundings for the first time. He had no idea how long Jeanne had been on her own, but the room was done in feminine pastel tones. There wasn't a lot of furniture, but the stuff looked fairly new. He wondered if she'd recently moved in or had redecorated with a new beginning in mind. He was sure there was no male influence here, just as his Los Angeles bungalow reflected no feminine touches. Emmett's apartment reflected his love of the theater. The jumble of heavy pieces he'd collected throughout the course of his marriage to Olivia, Ron's easygoing grandmother made it resemble the set of a gothic stage play.

The glittering Christmas tree set in the corner against the eggshell-colored drapes crossed all boundaries, and would have been a welcome addition to any home. It was a tree in the real spirit of Christmas, Ron realized with a lift. He was often in Europe at this time of year and had nothing but a miniature tabletop tree that he dragged out if he needed it. A genuine, full-bodied pine was such a pleasant sight after all these years. He wandered closer, shutting his eyes, inhaling its pungent scent, recapturing the childlike wonder of the holidays for a brief moment.

Then—*whop!* Ron flinched as something hit him between the shoulder blades. He looked down to find the purple foam ball bouncing between his feet. "Toby..." He turned slowly and found the boy had set up a miniature baseball diamond with four washcloths.

"C'mon, pitcha-pitcha!" Toby was standing in the oversize doorway beside a washcloth turned to form a diamond, a gigantic yellow bat in his hands. By the way he was wiggling it over his head, it had to be hollow, feather-light plastic. A child-size navy-blue Twins cap was jammed over his thick thatch of blond hair, and he was squinting at Ron from beneath the bill.

Ron bent over, picked up the ball, and tossed it several inches into the air. Should he?

"You a pitcha or belly itcha?" Toby taunted in a squeaky sort of growl.

Disguising a grin behind pursed lips, Ron ran his hand over the surface of his tan chamois shirt, gave his imaginery hat a tug, and stared down the batter. He didn't know the first thing about appeasing children, but he did remember exactly how to play schoolyard baseball. With a huge windmill wallop, he sent the sphere of foam across the diamond.

And the boy hit it. With a *thunk* it sailed the length of the living room. Ron tried to catch it in midair, but was thwarted by an end table. In the meantime, Toby ran the bases with his arms in the air.

The game went on for a good fifteen minutes. Toby finally gave Ron a turn at bat, but not until he'd tagged the boy out three times.

Ron couldn't resist the urge to hit. Caught up in the moment, the excitement, the roar of the crowd that Toby talked about, he went for broke. One good smack sent the ball soaring high, directly for the tree. With an outstretched arm Ron leaped to try and intercept it in flight. Toby made a grab for his belt loop and together they tumbled onto the carpeting. They didn't graze the tree by much, but it shook the pine in its red metal stand, sending a shower of tinsel and ornaments from its branches.

"Boys!"

Cradling Toby in his lap, Ron looked up to find Jeanne standing in the doorway near home plate, shaking the plastic bat like a wild hitter. A middle-aged woman, in striking makeup, was hovering in the foyer beyond, more than a little interested. He felt like a kid again, exhilarated, and slightly ashamed. "I am so sorry," he apologized, scrambling to his feet, aware that Toby was using him as a shield. "So very, very sorry."

Jeanne set the bat against the wall and turned her attention back to her customer. As she held out the woman's coat, complimenting her on her cashmere scarf, Ron realized Jeanne's face was hot with embarrassment. She must think him a maniac and he couldn't blame her.

"C'mon, sport," he whispered to the child. "Let's get these ornaments back in place."

No sooner did he have one wooden soldier hanging from a branch than Jeanne was back, alone and livid. "Toby, I want you to take care of this by yourself. I have business with Mr. Coleman."

"He said his name is Ron."

"And I'm happy to help," Ron assured her.

"I'll bet." She gazed at him knowingly. Anything to escape their showdown. "But we have business, remember?"

"Gravy dam," the boy muttered.

"What?" Ron appeared perplexed.

"Just a little something my sister told him." Jeanne's mouth softened as she crossed the room to place her hand on Toby's shoulder. "Put these things back on the tree."

"All by myself?" he squealed with a stomp of his tennis shoe.

"Yes!" Jeanne pointed a finger at Ron. "As for you, mister, come with me."

Raking his hands through his thatch of chestnut-brown hair, Ron obeyed.

Jeanne ushered him into her studio and closed the door firmly behind them.

"That's a great kid you have," he ventured.

"Yes, I know." She picked a strand of tinsel from his hair. She found it difficult to believe him capable of stringing her along again over the very same boy. But he was doing just that.

He chuckled suddenly. "I remember having to blow off some steam at that age, especially before Christmas."

"Yes, I understand *Toby,*" she said, putting clear emphasis on her son's name. "But he knows better. Baseball is a basement game around here."

"He probably just saw an opportunity for play and didn't think much further. Kids can be impetuous. I always was."

And always would be, most likely. Jeanne watched him move, the ripple of muscle in his back and thighs. Now that he'd admitted that he wasn't a Gracie's employee, she could see that the job wouldn't suit him at all. This man needed action. Lots of sharp-edged action. Why, his tanned skin alone was a dead giveaway. So who was he? Where did he fit in?

Ron knew she was sizing him up, and found it kind of a turn-on. With his hands clasped behind his back, he roamed the room with equal curiosity. "How clever, transforming this master bedroom into a work area."

"Yes, it's the biggest room in the house, and the bathroom comes in very handy. It's the perfect little beauty shop for my clients. You see, I don't just take photographs, I provide the hairdo, the makeup. The works."

His interest was piqued. "A fantasy kind of photo?"

"Yes."

"That woman looked stunning. You really must know your stuff."

"I studied cosmetology before my marriage, and have dabbled in photography since my gig on the high-school newspaper. After Toby was born, it was a way to supplement the family income while staying home with him. A hobby with some profits." She paused, again feeling she was blabbing too much.

"Seems like more than a hobby now," he remarked, respect in his voice. He knew something about the business and this was a bona fide studio. She had a twelve-foot-wide backdrop along one wall as well as a host of props which included a door, Gothic pillars, a bookshelf and a mock fireplace. There were three quality cameras visible, a tripod, and a variety of electronic flash equipment.

"I suddenly found myself the head of the household," she explained. "Got organized out of a sense of need more than anything else."

There were many more questions he longed to ask. How had she ended up this way? What had led her to transform her bedroom into her place of business? What had happened to her husband? Was her bed, wherever it was, empty?

Jeanne watched his expression grow pensive, and cursed her big mouth. Why was she opening up to this stranger?

Because he was interested, that's why. And she was flattered by his interest. No matter what sort of stunt he and Santa were trying to pull, Ron Coleman was tall, dark and handsome, and far sexier than anyone she'd ever run into buying groceries. Despite her irritation, she wanted to know more about him as well. "So, you're not part of the Grace's staff and their rebel Santa flat out refuses to see Toby?" she prompted.

"Afraid so." He smiled tightly, hooking his thumbs in his belt loops. "I may as well come clean here and now, Jeanne. I'm a journalist, not a salesman. And Emmett Windom is my eighty-year-old grandfather. I just happened to be at the North Pole when you showed up. I saw the chance to defuse a troublesome situation for Emmett and took it."

"So you *are* the other Ron Coleman!"

"There are two?"

"No, I guess not," she conceded. "But you are the famous one?"

"Yes."

"So our conversation—your side of it—was a complete waste of time." She gasped as the encounter replayed in her mind. "That was a mighty dirty trick, pretending to take my complaint seriously."

"Oh, I did take it seriously," he hastily and sincerely assured her. "Little else has been on my mind since. One conclusion I've reached is that we're in the same boat in many ways—"

"How can you say that!"

"We're both looking out for our own dream-chasing rascal, aren't we? When you think about it, my grandpa and your son have a lot of things in common—vulnerability, inflexibility, a tendency to throw tantrums!"

She absorbed the idea with a wry look. "What does this have to do with the Santa issue?"

"Everything, really. Toby believes in him and Emmett believes he is him!"

"You're putting me on."

"No." He shook his head emphatically. "Emmett's a dapper old stage performer, a student of the method-acting school. He's convinced that he *is* Santa while in costume. So confident that he's done the job right in the first place, he can't comprehend the idea of a retraction."

"Of all the Santas in the Cities to choose!" She threw up her hands. "So, in other words, you've simply come over here to give me the bad news in person."

"Well, I hoped to intercept you before you did return to Grace Brothers," he admitted. "Stanley Bickel, the manager of the store, is the real boss of Santa and is just looking for an excuse to fire Emmett. He has somebody else in mind for the job, you see."

She sighed. "Well, Emmett's certainly lucky to have such a protective grandson."

Encouraged by these words, Ron hurried to add, "He's really a wonderful old guy, but at his age, his eccentricities are locked in tight. If you'd just try to understand."

"Can you blame me for trying to make things right for Toby? He's pretty wonderful, too."

"Look, I'm trying to make it up to you. Losing this job would be the end of Emmett. Not only does it pay handsomely, but he needs to maintain his image in the theater community. When he goes for coffee on Grand Avenue, he needs to have new stories to tell his cronies. If he didn't have purpose, he'd whither away like an autumn leaf."

"He looked mighty sturdy to me," she argued. "And my mother said he was quite a flirt."

"Oh, he loves the ladies still." Ron smiled fondly.

Like Santa, like grandson, she couldn't help thinking.

"My folks watch over him as a rule, and they really have their hands full. Emmett's memory and eyes are failing a bit, but he still has the lusty drive to make things happen."

She smiled a little. "So you're just pinch-hitting, so to speak?"

"While my parents are vacationing in Arizona. I have a home in Los Angeles. It's nothing special. I'm on the road a lot, gathering material for books and articles."

"But you're from here, originally?"

Ron knew Minnesotans, unlike transplanted Californians, always liked to hear about local roots. He couldn't help thinking how similar Jeanne was to the girls he used to date in school. Fresh, centered, generous. "Absolutely. I was raised on the south side of Minneapolis."

"Well, I think it's wonderful that a busy guy like you cares enough about his grandfather to come home and—"

"I do care. And you'd like him too, once you got to know him." He stepped closer to her, a dazzling smile of encouragement on his face. "Please reconsider, Jeanne, and accept the gift certificate for Grace Brothers in the spirit it was given."

"No, I won't!" She crossed the room to a small desk near the door and picked up the bright red-and-green envelope lying atop a heap of business papers. She whirled around to find he'd followed her. They collided with a thump.

Just as he'd planned, of course. He'd inherited enough of Emmett's acting ability to look suitably surprised, before sniffing her soft, fair head. "Mmm, lemon shampoo. My favorite."

Spicy masculine scent. A long-forgotten favorite of hers. She self-consciously realized that her nose was pressed into the softness of his chamois shirt. And she was enjoying it. Too much.

"Can't we be adult about this?" he asked huskily.

She tipped her face up to his, her brilliant blue eyes dancing suspiciously. "What do you mean?"

"Christmas is strictly for old folks and children, isn't it? The dreams, the tradition."

"And in what spirit was this gift certificate given?"

"The spirit of survival?" he replied with good humor.

"Oh, so this Christmas fuss is just an inconvenience to you?" she asked, assessing his position with dead accuracy.

"Well, yeah. It was super at Toby's age, of course. But at this stage of my life, I feel differently."

"Self-absorbed Reporter Plays Hero, Dragging Boy and his Santa Through the Holidays on a Rusty Sled." She fired out the words like a bold headline reporting a tragedy.

"That's about the size of it," he said with thinning patience. "I thought you'd agree, with all the stress you seem to be under."

She didn't answer immediately, and when she spoke, her voice was cold and distant. "Why, I almost believed you were..."

"Were what?" he demanded in bewilderment.

"A holiday junkie like me," she admitted disappointedly.

He inhaled in sharp surprise. He'd mucked this up even further it seemed. She was harried about her holiday obligations, but apparently enjoyed the condition. It seemed the harder he tried to please her, the closer the foot in his mouth came to nudging his tonsils. "Isn't it enough that I'm taking the blame on Emmett's behalf?" he asked. "That I want to pick up the tab?"

She regarded him with disgust. "So, life in your mind is one big tab?"

How quickly she could cut to the chase. "Hey, I didn't invent the policy, I just go with the flow. This seems so cut-and-dried to me."

"Have you ever been married? Have any children?"

"No."

"I didn't think so. Cut-and-dried," she sputtered. "You must get up close and personal on those news stories with nothing shorter than a ten-foot pen!"

The professional insult angered him, especially since he doubted she'd ever read any of his stuff. "I can understand a person's point of view, and report on it with insight."

She made a doubtful sound. "Nothing makes up for experience, something you seem to be lacking big-time."

That gibe, too, struck home. Gravy darn, it did. He wasn't accustomed to being unmasked or riled. Ron's eyes traveled round the room as he sought a comeback, something brilliant and unimpeachable. He gasped as he spied a large wall clock near the door. "That isn't really the time, is it?"

"Yes. Twelve-fifteen."

"I have to go. Emmett can't be late for work." He seized her by the arms so suddenly she gasped. "Please promise not to follow me."

She made an incredulous sound. "What!"

"Back to the store I mean, to play the tattletale. Give me some time, and I'll sort this out for Toby."

She shook her head as he dashed out of the studio. Sort things out? There had been blind panic in his eyes when she'd challenged his skills and sentiment. Why, he couldn't hope to sort his way out of a gift-wrapped package!

"ONE NIGHT ON your own, Ron, and you're sitting in the dark with your diary." Emmett strode into the living room and stood in the glow from the streetlight outside the window.

"Hi, Pop." Ron shifted in the dilapidated chair of crushed rust velvet and oak that Emmett once gleaned from a *Hamlet* production. "I keep telling you, it's a journal, not a diary."

"Right. Tough guys don't do diaries. Even the toughest switch on a light, though." Emmett moved around the room, clicking lamps to life. His black topcoat, resting on his shoulders, trailed out behind him as he moved.

Ron stifled a yawn. "It was light when I sat down. Guess I dozed off."

"Appears you actually wrote something tonight," Emmett observed dryly. "That's a switch."

Ron flipped the book shut in a gesture of self-defense. "Venting my frustrations, I guess. So how was your evening?"

Emmett whisked off his coat and put it in the closet. "Dating women in the fifty- sixty-year range is such an inspiration," he rejoiced smugly. "They're still quite pretty and have the temperaments of angels. Tonight's granny picked me up right at the store, then wheeled us around town with dexterity and remarkable night vision."

"Going to see her again?"

"Indeed. She's picking me up at Grace Brothers after work tomorrow, then we're on to a choir concert at her church." He moved to a rocker opposite Ron that he'd acquired from a *Death of a Salesman* set. "So how is our pretty little mother managing?"

"Fuming. Still refuses to take that gift certificate."

The lines around Emmett's mouth deepened. "A matter of pride?"

"Yeah, I think the outright charity of it made her uncomfortable."

Emmett sighed. "That's too bad. Thanks for the effort, though. It was good of you to try, to care so much about the old man."

Ron was frustrated by resignation. "It isn't over by a long shot. I still have to resolve this somehow. Stop her from turning you in."

"She may have been tempted to report me," his grandfather said calmly, "but I think it was a bluff. As I said earlier, she's a lady of discrimination. I could tell by her voice. Beautiful diction, with an underlying charm."

"You do know voices, Pop, I grant you—"

"And now we know that she's not the type to grab an exorbitant payoff—even if it is one you could well afford. Another example of good character."

Ron set his journal on the end table, then leaned forward earnestly. "She's as down-to-earth as you can imagine. Runs a photography studio out of her home while taking care of her turbocharged boy. But you've got to understand. She is a protective mother first and foremost, who takes the role very seriously." Ron used the term deliberately. Emmett understood roles.

"I'd say the child is a lucky lad." Emmett pursed his lips in thought.

"She will put his holiday happiness way above your job security," Ron warned him.

"Well, in any case, I feel you gave it your best shot. Time to let Fate take it's course."

"I can't believe you're willing to run this risk!"

"I can handle myself, Ron, really." Emmett's old eyes hardened.

"Sure you can—"

"Are you?" His tone sharpened a fraction. "I expect Bernice will always fuss over me because she's my only child, daddy's girl. And you see me through her eyes a lot of the time because she's often the bridge between us. How's Grandpa doing? How's Grandson doing? We ask her and she makes the judgment calls."

Ron clasped his hands together. "Guess that's true to a point."

"I see myself in a realistic light always, despite what you and your mother think." When Ron's brows rose skeptically, he chuckled. "I'm an aging performer who still likes to wring out a solid performance from the depths of my soul. True, I forget things and take ginger steps in the snow and the shower. But I can still handle Stanley Bickel!" he bellowed with a shaking fist. "Even if Jeanne Trent does her damnest, I have a defense. You know as well as anyone there has not been another single complaint."

Ron swallowed hard. When he spoke, his voice was husky. "I guess there's no reason to pursue the issue any further, then."

"You sound disappointed."

"Do I?"

Emmett's mouth curled mockingly. "Yes, as though my dilemma was just so much fun and now it's over."

Ron flushed. "Begging beautiful women for mercy isn't my idea of fun. You know how tough it is to beg?" he demanded plaintively.

The rail-thin man shivered beneath his dress clothes, as though repelled by the idea. "Can't say I do. Never been a beggar myself."

"Bickering too," Ron complained. "Bickering and begging. All for you!"

Emmett rose stiffly and stretched his arms above his head. "Always have enjoyed a good bicker with a hot-blooded woman. More than a few ended up begging in the end," he quipped, highly amused.

Ron smiled thinly. Emmett's love life sounded more fruitful and fertile with every passing year. It was amazing how the man could manipulate his own memories for entertainment purposes. "Just trying to help you, Pop. Seems only right you should cooperate."

"Really?" Emmett stood over him, his spine erect and his chin high, the imposing father figure suddenly. "I feel I must be honest for your own good, Ronny. We've always had a special bond, two headstrong fellows bent on avoiding the mundane at all costs. As much as I enjoy your visits, the camaraderie renewed..." He hesitated, weighing his words. "I can't help but feel you might be using me as some sort of excuse this time around."

"What!" Ron's strong jaw slackened.

"I'm not challenging your goodwill, but you are behaving strangely."

"How?"

"You're characteristically full of yourself when you come, hearty and sure, talking a mile a minute about life and your footloose cronies."

"Good lord, that's a description of you!"

Emmett's chest puffed like a rooster's. "Yes, and a flattering one. Furthermore, you're usually pounding away on that laptop contraption of yours about some adventure you've had or stolen from somebody else. This time, aside from tonight, you seem at a loss for words, and obsessively focused on me, as though I'm some kind of geriatric pet project." The idea obviously left a bad taste in his mouth.

"I'll back off a little," Ron grumbled, studying his laced fingers.

"That isn't enough! I'm telling you to dig, Ronny. Examine your motives. Perhaps you feel at a crossroads, son," he suggested. "You're thirty now, without a family, a clear direction, a significant other to run hot water for your feet."

Ron's mouth twitched then. Foot-soaking was a pleasure more suited to Emmett's advanced age. Ron had no trouble suppressing his glee, however. The picture Emmett had painted of him was all too accurate. How shrewd of the old man to put all the pieces together. Ron knew he was looking for purpose in his overbearing care of Emmett. He'd come back to hometown comfort hoping to recharge his creative batteries.

But he'd die before admitting it outright.

Emmett reached out to ruffle Ron's brown head the way he used to years ago. "Jeanne Trent is quite pretty and seems worth knowing. Is it possible that saving my job is only part of your motive for pursuing her? Could it be that you enjoyed meeting the lady yourself and hoped to milk it a little longer, using my plight as a front?"

"Even if I did try and pull that sort of stunt, she ended up hurling insults at me with your kind of skill. That's hard to take from a female a guy barely knows."

Emmett smiled blandly. "A little bickering and begging with the right lady may be just what you need."

Ron's self-control slipped. "She was brutal." He went on to repeat Jeanne's crack about the ten-foot pen. "I'm not an impostor, Pop. I've delivered the goods. Seen life and reported it!"

"Oh, I know, son. You've had tremendous success. Did you try to tell her?"

"Didn't have the time. Had to come back for you."

"You're just bound and determined to blame all your troubles on me, aren't you?" Ron couldn't bear the unmistakable hurt in Emmett's faded eyes.

"You're trouble for sure, Pop," he said gently. "But I definitely botched things up myself. I came across as a crass wise guy about Christmas, with the gift-certificate push and some other blundering remarks."

Emmett nodded his silver head in understanding. "A holiday that presumably means something to her."

"Oh, yes. Huge tree, lavish decorations throughout the house. The sort of thing Mom and Dad delivered throughout my childhood."

Ron's interest in Jeanne was disguised by the flimsiest of veils now. So was Emmett's disgust. "Then the visual signs were there, Ron. Why did you make yourself look like a globe-trotting grinch right out of the bull pen?"

Ron had given that question a great deal of thought. "Maybe I was hoping she'd try and convince me I was wrong," he suggested.

"She was to do all that? Hardly knowing you? With concerns of her own?"

"She could have," Ron argued. Despite her spunky stand, her qualities had shone through like the brightest ornament imaginable. He'd found her sassy, sexy, exciting. Why couldn't she have reciprocated?

Ron sat in sulky silence. Gravy dam, leave it to Emmett the tireless interrogator to dredge it all up.

"The Trent house sounds like a mighty nice place to be at Christmas," Emmett murmured, shuffling toward the hallway. "No, I'm not going to worry for one minute about her son's interests. That woman, she knows exactly how to make wishes come true." Lifting a hand, he disappeared.

Ron had come to a similar conclusion. Jeanne's warm Christmas cottage was storybook inviting. Visions of her soft smile and feminine curves danced in his head like sugarplums, making him yearn for a place at her place.

But it was ridiculous to dream this way. A five-year-old fruitcake, run over by a mail truck, would be more welcome at her door!

4

"GRACE BROTHERS does not return cash on this kind of transaction, sir."

Ron stared at the prim female clerk behind the store's customer service counter Wednesday afternoon, tapping his three-hundred-dollar certificate on the glass surface between them. The red-and-green striped envelope was looking a little dog-eared and so was he. The idea of getting his money back with a dash of charisma had seemed like a cinch in theory, just as buying off Jeanne had. At first...

He was amazed as well as horrified by his circumstances. This retreat back into his wintry hometown had his nerves frayed to the limit. His visions of sitting by cozy fires with good books and wines were gone, along with the ice skates he'd imagined strapped to his feet as he'd skimmed across one of Minnesota's ten thousand lakes.

There seemed little doubt left. Not only was he flat out of inspiration, but it seemed he'd lost all appeal to the opposite sex.

But in his own defense, this clerk was more up Emmett's alley, right down to the name tag bearing the name Lenora. Emmett liked names that rolled grandly off the tongue. She wore a simple lilac dress most likely all the rage back in the fifties, and had a cap of steel-gray hair slightly longer than his own. He cast Emmett a beseeching look over his shoulder. Where was the old actor's magic when it could be truly useful?

Emmett's hand pressed against the leather sleeve of Ron's jacket, signaling caution. "Couldn't you make an exception in Ron's case?"

Lenora's pale blue eyes hardened. "Listen, Hamlet," she snapped flatly, "I've manned this counter for thirty years, since the day Wendell and Arnold Grace themselves cut the ribbon to the front doors. Gift certificates are nonrefundable."

"I've been a friend of the Grace boys myself for even longer, you fussbudget," Emmett said loftily, his nostrils flared like a wild stallion's.

Lenora stepped back dramatically. "Deary me, you've bothered to make male chums along the way? When would you have had the time, you—you Santa Claus Casanova!"

Ron rolled his eyes. The name-calling suggested the worst: Lenora was a woman scorned, and intent on punishing Emmett for it. As Ron looked around the huge bustling store, he realized she would have a clear view of Santa's throne from here, and be able to watch Emmett's flirty antics. Unexpectedly, his grandfather's backup was sinking any chance of getting around the policy so boldy printed on a sign against the wall, right beneath a pledge of friendly service.

Mistaking Ron's thoughtful pause for his cue, Emmett suddenly shoved him aside, and leaned over the countertop until his head was close to Lenora's angry face.

"The name is Emmett," he hissed. "When I am dressed in street clothes I expect to be addressed as such. Or Mr. Windom, if you prefer."

"I prefer that you remove yourself from my sight," she returned huffily.

"That I can do!" With a flourish he removed the coat draped across his shoulders, and tossed it over his arm. "Just to clear up any misunderstandings or hard feelings," he said on a gentler note, "I feel it only fair to confess that I date only younger women."

Lenora's long bony fingers flew up in the air in mocking surprise. "Good heavens, Methuselah, we're *all* younger than you!"

With a single sniff worthy of a thousand retorts, Emmett marched down the center aisle toward the employees' lounge.

Ron affected an amused chuckle as he turned back to Lenora. "You just gotta love the eccentric old guy, don't you?"

"I don't gotta," she fumed. "Just as I don't gotta give you a refund."

"Look," he said quietly, "a goodwill gesture fell through for me. Having no children of my own, or nieces or nephews, I've no use for the kind of merchandise you handle."

"I must say, you do seem like a fine young man," she admitted with gruff sincerity, "putting up with him and all. But I can't see my way clear to bending the rules this time."

Ron sighed heavily. "Emmett's the decider, isn't he? You just can't bring yourself to give him the satisfaction." Her stoic silence confirmed it. "How about we keep it a secret, just between the two of us."

Resting her elbow on the counter, she crooked her finger at him. He leaned over, boyish hope in his features. "All I can give you is some advice. Next time, drop the old buzzard. He doesn't do a thing for your image."

Ron closed his eyes with a solemn nod. "So what do you suggest I do about this certificate?"

"Shop till you drop." With an abrupt motion she pushed herself away from the counter to answer a ringing telephone.

Ron tried. Braving the crowded aisles, he surveyed row upon row of every conceivable kind of toy. Dolls that wet, dinosaurs that roared, planes that flew, cars that honked. He craned his neck every which way in the gigantic building, even upward, to the stuffed animals hanging from the ceiling.

He eventually bumped into Emmett in full costume as the old man made his way to the North Pole on the heels of two perky elves and the store photographer, a plump redhead in her early twenties. Ron suspected that the redhead had little interest in the art of photography by the careless way she handled the equipment. Naturally he couldn't help but think of Jeanne and her passion for the same kind of work. Her passions in general. He hadn't been so captivated by a woman in a very long time.

"Any luck with our store bully, Ron?" Emmett asked, breaking into his musings.

Realizing adoring eyes were already on Santa Claus, Ron kept a frozen smile. "No," he said between his teeth. "Told me to shop till I drop. Unfair, when all she really wants is for you to drop dead. Didn't you have any idea she was harboring a secret crush?"

Emmett was aghast. "Certainly not!"

Ron's eyes widened skeptically. "Her infatuation would be obvious to anyone. Admit to me that she was harboring a grudge. That playing sentinel behind me wasn't a good idea."

"How preposterous."

"That exercise in egotism cost me three hundred smackers!"

"Well, just call me the ghost of your Christmas Future," his grandfather retorted with a measure of pride. "We're so much alike...it's as if you're a walking tribute to me."

Ron studied him grimly. "Then maybe we're both in big trouble."

"Huh?" Emmett was about to ask what Ron meant by that cryptic remark when he noted parents and toddlers closing ranks on the Pole. "Ho-ho-ho, son!" he bellowed with a jolly belly laugh. "What would you like for Christmas?"

Ron patted the shoulder of Santa's red jacket. "Let you know, old-timer," he said in a loud, jovial voice.

"Better to give than receive," Santa proclaimed. He got the expected round of applause.

Ron's eyes gleamed mischievously. "Yeah, I would like to see you get it. Which gives me an idea. Think I'll shop for you here. Right here and now."

Emmett's eyes grew wide in panic. "I want a new VCR, you know that, Ronny."

"That's boring," Ron whispered tauntingly. "You hate boring."

Emmett's lips curled over his beard as he mounted the white glittery steps to his carved mahogany chair.

Ron began to scour the store with determination. Surely there was something in the place that Emmett could use in his apartment, something that would antagonize him. Perhaps a small pool in which to soak his feet. He found a wading-sized one and paraded it past the Pole. When he caught Emmett's attention, he gestured to the pool, and his shoes.

"No-ho-ho!" Emmett proclaimed heartily, before turning back to mug for the camera and the fidgety little girl on his knee.

Ron went through the ritual several times. He passed by the Pole with a giant wall clock framed with a bright yellow sunburst, then a shoe rack in the shape of a monkey, and finally a Mickey Mouse telephone. Emmett declined them all from his kingly perch with a shower of no-hos.

Ron strolled through the game aisle, wondering if there was some little gadget he could take on his plane trips. With hands shoved in the pockets of his leather jacket he stared at the stacks of boxes on the shelves. Children of preschool age were swarming around him like the residents of a huge ant farm, their small hands tearing treasures off the shelves for inspection. It had to be a toddler trait to settle on the floor with a bottom bouncing plop, because that's what so many of them did—as Toby had while the two of them scooped up the ornaments that had toppled from Jeanne's perfect tree.

A boy about Toby's size was seated at his left, playing with some kind of pinball game. Ron stared down to watch the metal marbles rolling and rattling inside a clear plastic box housing a baseball diamond.

An inspiration suddenly hit him. "Is that fun?"

The child tipped his freckled face up. "Yup."

Man and boy turned as a faded-looking woman about Ron's age rushed through the crowd, with a cart holding two other children. She met Ron's eyes for a stricken moment, then dropped her lashes like a shield. No question, he'd lost his touch with women. Why, he couldn't even blame Emmett for this one's lack of interest.

"Just playin', Mommy," the boy whined as the woman tugged him to his feet.

"You aren't supposed to wander off!"

The boy sidled up close to her with a sigh. "Sorry."

The mother looked at Ron again with nervous little glances, as though he was some kind of weirdo.

"I was, ah, just wondering about the game he was playing," Ron assured her with a gentle smile. "Had the idea to buy it for another little boy I know."

"You don't have a child, do you?" She asked the question abruptly, then pinched her lips together.

Realization dawned on him as he scanned her plain, cosmetic-free face, her pale, limp hairdo. She wasn't afraid he was a creep at all. She feared that he might recognize her! "Elaine," he said softly.

"Yes," she admitted with a spurt of laughter. "It's me all right."

His smile grew, a blend of pleasure and sheepishness. He'd made a choice after high school. Life with Elaine at the University of Minnesota, or a solo trip to UCLA. Thirsty for adventure he had chosen the solo trip. Elaine hadn't taken it well at the time, and had hooked up with a football jock even before he'd set out for California. Tony. Tony Rosetti, if memory served him. "Been a while, hasn't it?" he finally said carefully, aware that her eyes were swimming with emotion.

She laughed again. "Twelve years, come this summer."

"Three children." They were all dark, like Tony. What would they look like if he had been their father?

"Actually, Tony and I have five children," she said with forced gaiety. "Two older boys are in school."

"All boys," he noted, grinning at the bunch.

"Yes. A girl would've been fun, of course," she said awkwardly.

"You always did enjoy dolling up," he recalled fondly. "That little girl would've been—" He paused in midsentence, as a shadow darkened her green eyes. "Would've been nice." He'd been about to remark that the child would've been dressed like a princess. But that was unlikely, judging by the worn jackets they were all wearing.

It was obvious that Elaine's primping days were long gone. She was no longer a self-absorbed teenager, but rather a busy housewife, presumably budgeting money and hours to her family's best advantage. How hard this must be for her, to run into him this way, unprepared. Elaine was still lovely, but by the way she was moving her bare lips together, as though smoothing a new coat of lipstick, she felt dowdy at the moment.

"I still think of you sometimes," he admitted softly. "Wonder if you're happy."

"Really?" she lilted, relaxing a little. "Well, I am. We have all the regular problems, you know, over finances and kid stuff. But Tony and the kids are my life. They give me an indescribable feeling of fulfillment."

"Mommy, Bobby's nose!" The boy who'd been fascinated by the pinball game was gesturing to the baby in the cart.

Elaine swiftly produced a tissue from her purse and dabbed the child's lip. "To you this must seem so dull, with all your adventures, the women you must know."

"Oh, I don't know," he murmured. And it was a true statement! He just didn't know. In spite of all his travels and accomplishments he was currently as confused as an adolescent.

"Read your books of course," she said. "And enjoyed them. I could hear your voice so clearly. First-person-singular suits your writing."

"Thanks. I appreciate the fact that you can still stand the sound of my voice."

"Oh, Ron." She sighed in affectionate exasperation. "No hard feelings anymore, really."

"I'm glad. And if it means anything to you, Laine, I'm beginning to wonder if I ever should've left town—and you—in the first place."

She gasped in disbelief, flushing prettily in a way no makeup could match. "Of course you should have! You'd never have been satisfied with settling down back then. You had to...discover things."

She'd given their relationship a lot of thought, he realized. Presumably to work through his rejection. "So, how is Tony?"

"Oh, fine, just fine," she assured him. "He and a friend opened up a small service station in North Minneapolis, in our old neighborhood. Just a few pumps. They plan to focus mainly on repairs."

"He always did dream of having his own shop," Ron recalled suddenly.

"Yes, and his dreams were put on hold for quite some time. It's a huge risk for us, but he deserves his chance. So, what are you doing in St. Paul anyway?" she asked on a lighter note. "So far from Los Angeles. Heck, it's even far from our old turf."

"You remember my grandpa, don't you? He's settled here in St. Paul now."

"Emmett?" Her smile widened. "Why, I've often wondered if he's still on stage."

He tipped his head in the direction of the North Pole. "The most beloved role of all," he said cryptically, so as to not alert the children.

"Really? What a small world it is!"

"You really should go see him. He'd be delighted."

"All right. We'll stop. The kids will love it."

He touched the hand she'd curled around the cart handle. "It was so nice to see you again, Laine."

Elaine inhaled unsteadily. "Darn you for not behaving like everybody else! Showing up at the class reunions when a girl's at her best."

"You're the best anyplace, anytime. Take care now."

Ron turned to take a pinball game off the shelf and wended his way to the front of the store. Lenora was helping someone else as he stepped up to the service desk, so he patiently waited his turn.

"Knew you'd be back," she purred triumphantly, sliding her pen into the wedge of gray hair above her ear. "And if you want my opinion, I'd say the wading pool best suited the old boy."

"Good for soaking things," Ron agreed. "Feet, heads, egos."

Lenora laughed pleasantly. Ron wondered why Emmett hadn't noticed her qualities. She was bright, efficient and attractive. A tiger when riled. What more could Pop want?

"I'm afraid I'm going to have to disappoint you again," she clucked.

"How so, Lenora?"

"You wish to buy that item and get about two hundred and eighty dollars in currency, don't you?"

He might have, ten minutes ago. But life was slapping sense into him at every turn. "Not at all," he said, feigning hurt.

"Well, good, because here at Grace Brothers we just whack the purchase off the certificate. You'd still be running a tab."

"I'm going to pay cash for this," he told her, enjoying her surprise.

"What's up your sleeve?"

"Patience, Lenora. First, I want you to look back at the North Pole for me."

"Why?"

As if she didn't do it a hundred times a day on her own! "Just because. Please?"

Lenora sized up the Pole over her reading glasses. "All I see is a windbag in the red suit."

"There's something more to see," he urged, slipping his hand into the lining pocket of his jacket for his wallet. "A woman with three children. She's wearing a coral coat—"

"Oh, yes, at the end of the line. Somebody special?"

Hmm, nosy like Emmett, too.

"Oops, she's looking back at me."

"Then look away," he whispered in distress. "Play along, please."

"I have a job to do here," she protested halfheartedly. "If you'd get to the point."

"Okay, okay." He produced the red-and-green envelope again. "I would deeply appreciate it you'd award this to that lady."

Her long fingers fluttered. "How? For what?"

"Oh, I don't know, for having the brightest coat! Doesn't matter much. She's got five sons and isn't going to examine your motives too thoroughly." He made an exasperated sound. "Don't you see? It would get spent and settle the matter."

Her eyes searched his face, then she nodded. "You're trying to do something nice, I can see that. But we don't have policies for this kind of thing."

"Thirty years at your post surely give you the freedom to rig policy," he argued. "Especially at Christmas."

"You're right," she relented, flattered. "I can do it and I will." She snatched up the certificate. "But you are leaving now, aren't you? It's only fair that I serve other customers some time today, too."

"Consider me kin to the wind," he said airily.

She laughed then, a lyrical sound that turned employees' heads in wonder. "Now blow before I change my mind."

IT WAS ABOUT two-thirty that afternoon when Ron eased his burgundy rental car to a stop in front of the Trents' one-story brick house. Like most of the other homes on the street, hers was shaped like a shoe box. But it was adorned with extras that set it apart; white window boxes and shutters, a handrail on the concrete stoop, new-looking gutters edging the roof.

Jeanne dressed in her blue parka and jeans, was the most eye-catching adornment.

It had snowed heavily during the night and she was in the process of shoveling her sidewalk and stoop. She was nearly finished; only one step remained snow covered.

Though she didn't turn immediately, Ron knew she had heard the slamming of the car door and the click of his heels on the concrete path. She was holding her body alertly, like a sleek and beautiful cat. He envisioned her turning to discover the man she adored, dropping her shovel, running at full tilt, then bowling him over in the snow and smothering him with kisses.

He stumbled a little on a slippery patch, his pulse pounding as he imagined being that man. Oh, how he wanted to be here. How he yearned to be wanted by this woman. How he would manage to become part of her life he didn't know, but one obstacle had been hurdled. He'd found the guts to return.

Ron was so absorbed by these thoughts, he didn't notice exactly when she really turned to face him. She was now leaning on the handle of her shovel, regarding him with a wry expression.

"You're back."

"Yeah."

"I wasn't expecting you."

Naturally not. He was as surprised by this visit as she! He'd even fought the urge to return for a couple of hours after leaving Grace Brothers. Ultimately, in spite of the fact that he knew he wouldn't be welcome, he simply couldn't stay away.

It was seeing Elaine that had done it. It had been twelve years since he'd left Elaine for California and adventure, and in all that time he had never found another woman like her. Until now. After he'd left the store he'd come to the sudden, disturbing realization that Jeanne was more appealing to him than Elaine had ever been.

Jeanne, not having had the same revelation, was annoyed and suspicious. But awaiting his reply just the same. If he had to settle for curiosity at this juncture, he would.

"I said I'd sort things out for Toby," he ventured confidently.

Her slim brows rose speculatively. "Have you?"

"Uh, the plan is in progress." He held up the sack. "For now, I did come across something I think he might like—"

"Ten days before Christmas, Ron?" She gave a snort of derision. "What an amateur you are!"

He stalked up to the bottom of the stoop. "Hey, I know how the process works. I was a kid once myself."

Her mouth crooked in a smile. "Grown up since the tree-bouncing baseball game yesterday, have you?"

"That was an accident," he said defensively. "Actually, this toy is a gift to you in a way, something to slow Toby down." He dropped his car keys in his jacket pocket and fumbled with the bag. The slippery plastic was like liquid butter in his huge, chilled hands. "Whoa!" He nearly dropped the works into the snow.

Her spontaneous laughter filled the air as she rested her shovel against the house. "Come inside, Mr. California, before you land on your butt."

"The older I get, the quicker I freeze up in the arctic air," he said, trailing after her into the warm holly-trimmed foyer.

"Your ears are certainly red," she noted. "You need a cap."

He would rather she concentrated on his butt, but would have to take things in the order they came. Did she have any idea how appealing she was with that furry hood circling her heart-shaped face, her full lips parted with humor? She peeled off her outer clothes and invited him to do the same. He handed her the package, eased off his jacket, and hung it on a peg inside the closet door.

She peered inside the bag. "Toby's napping right now."

"Perfect time to take a look at that and see what you think," he suggested.

She looked at him gratefully as she held the box lengthwise in her hands. "This was a good idea. Might appease him until he can take his game outside."

"Good. Then you'll keep it."

"Yes, thanks." She drew a hesitant breath. "Would you like a cup of coffee?"

"Very much."

She set a plate of Christmas cookies out on the table as well and he wolfed them down. His stomach had been so tight over this visit that he hadn't stopped for lunch. Now that he was with her again he was ravenous.

Ron swallowed self-consciously, aware that she was studying him intently. "You're staring," he said mildly. "With eyes glazed over in shock."

Jeanne's wind-flushed face grew a trifle rosier as she busily raised her steamy mug to her lips. She was staring because she was half-certain he was an apparition. Not since David had a dynamic man sat with her at this table. He was trying to play it cool, but she could see the vulnerability and interest in his expression.

"Sorry," she said laughing. "I really wasn't expecting you back."

She had the sudden, irresistible urge to make sure he was flesh and not some little diversion she'd created for herself. With as much grace as possible she reached out and grazed her forefinger along the cleft in his chin. "There! That takes care of the sugar." And her doubts. He was the real thing, all right. Her fingertip was on fire. And the heat was slowly spreading, giving her a sexy and desired feeling.

"I didn't handle myself very well yesterday, roughhousing with Toby," he admitted, shifting on the smooth chair as lightning coursed through his veins. He hadn't expected her to touch him without warning. That was one of his old tricks! He cleared his throat, struggling with his composure. "Guess I got carried away."

"Well, it suggested that you do like Christmas a little more than you were letting on," she said pleasantly. "Or did, once upon a time."

"Yeah, guess those feelings have faded some over the years." He looked around the cheery, cluttered kitchen with a smile. "Your house reminds me of my folks' place in North Minneapolis. And, well, Toby reminds me of myself at that age."

Her blue eyes twinkled. "Bet I would've liked you a lot back then."

But what about now? The question bounced around the confines of his hollow heart.

"I have to take part of the blame for our quarrels," she went on. "I've gone over things in my mind and see how you could've gotten the impression that I might settle for a payoff. I did talk of budgets, affording things. It's true as far as it goes. . . ." She trailed off uncomfortably.

He raised a hand. "All that should matter is that I want to make up for Emmett's stunt."

"But your grandfather is the only person who can right this situation."

"I refuse to accept that," Ron argued. "Toby liked me, too."

She tucked her blond tresses behind her ears and nodded in slow affirmation. "I have to admit he hasn't stopped talking about you since yesterday."

"Surely together we can—" He stopped short. For just a second, before she lowered her lashes, he saw longing in her eyes. Was she envisioning the two of them together, on an intimate level, as he had outside? "Together we can bamboozle one little boy into believing Santa's come through," he finished brightly. "Can't we?"

"I really don't see how," she said, nibbling on a bell-shaped cookie. "It's complicated."

"Please tell me about it," he urged quietly. "I want to understand."

She shrugged her thin shoulders, and continued to hide her eyes beneath her lush lashes. "This is our first Christmas without my late husband David. Despite his young age, Toby does remember last year, the fun we all had."

Ron absorbed this new insight. No wonder he was such a little pistol! "He's having fun with the holiday, Jeanne. It's obvious."

"I know he is, so far. But if something goes wrong, this first Christmas after David's passing, he may forever feel sad at this time of year. It's certainly the last thing David would've wanted."

Her compassion and her distress overwhelmed him. "Children his age aren't that tough to satisfy, are they? He may not even remember every single thing he asked for."

"Ron, if Toby made some sort of request concerning his father, he's going to remember."

"Oh, my Lord," he moaned. He rubbed his face in his hands.

"The last thing I'm looking for is sympathy," she hastily assured him. "I've had a truckload. I'm in the process of rebuilding, looking ahead."

The news excited him. She wasn't going to crumble and she was available. He struggled to keep his voice even and his manner patient as he waded further into personal territory. "What happened to your husband? Do you mind talking about it?"

She smiled sadly. "David died last January in a single-car crash. He was on his way home from work one evening and had stopped on Rice Street for Chinese takeout. The weather was bad. It was snowing, the roads were icy. Anyway, he took one of the curves on Wheelock Parkway a little too sharply and lost control. Hit a tree. Died instantly, they said."

Her voice had become a monotone and the way she related incident sounded a bit like a recitation. He realized it was a shield against her emotions, a way to relate the tragedy from a safe distance. He'd seen it hundreds of times in his work.

"Bet this year's been rough."

"Yes," she agreed breathlessly. "But I couldn't fall apart, you see. For one thing, Potters—my family—just don't do that. We're too eccentric, too strong. And I constantly reminded myself that Toby deserved a mother running on all cylinders." She laced her fingers around her mug and smiled. "Anyhow, the situation today is that we're at the tail end of enduring a year's worth of milestones without David. The Christmas holidays are the last. I feel if I can just fulfill Toby's most important wishes and convince my suffocating family that I'm fine... Well, that's what I want for Christmas this year!"

"It sure would help to know what he wants most," Ron sympathized. "Funny, most kids can't stop talking about it, can they?"

"Toby is a bit of a tease," she replied. "He likes to put me in tight corners."

Ron stroked his jaw, hoping to conceal his twitching mouth. He and Toby had things in common, no question. "If we could just wheedle that list out of him, find out what we're dealing with."

Jeanne was overwhelmed with a fresh wave of warmth. *We.* He kept adding himself to the picture. And did it so naturally, with a deep, soothing baritone that no doubt had women opening up in all sorts of ways. "These are the times when I miss David most," she blurted out. "When I need a partner to outwit that child!"

"So how long were you married?" he asked gently.

She gazed at him mutely, her temperature on the rise again. When was this confirmed bachelor going to flip back to his self-centered self again? She was more comfortable with that side of him. He was easier to battle, easier to dismiss. Maybe if she refused to answer any more personal questions, he would storm out. "Seven years," she heard herself say in a wispy way no aggressive Potter would even recognize!

"High-school romance?"

"Yes. Puppy love that grew into something deep and adult." She studied her nails with a brief smile. "We seemed to belong together right from the start."

"A lot of Christmases clocked in, I imagine."

"Wonderful ones." She propped her chin in her hand and studied him curiously. "So tell me more about you."

"Like what?"

"Like your Christmases, for instance."

"Well, once upon a time they were full of tradition like yours," he replied. "My youth was great in general, really.

I'm an only child who was probably spoiled a little. My parents are normal, the kind other kids like to talk to."

"So how did you ever escape Minneapolis in the first place?"

His chocolate-colored eyes twinkled teasingly. "Well, the folks made the mistake of encouraging me to think too big—or so they say now that I haven't married and reproduced. Seriously though, I grew restless during high school and longed for more. I headed for Los Angeles and beyond."

"Did you find more? Out there?"

"Oh, yes." He stared out the window facing the backyard, and spied a gigantic snowman. "Always a new rainbow to chase. Wrote all about it."

"Did you eventually find your pot of gold?"

He continued to stare at the snowman. "I guess the treasure is relative. Guess we know for sure when we stop digging for it."

"Or running from it." The words popped out of her mouth before she could stop them. "I meant that in a general way, really."

He slowly swiveled to face her. She was backpedaling to save his feelings. But it was no less than he deserved. The way he'd swooped in to play Emmett's diplomatic deputy with egotistical gusto, he must seem like a shallow, careless playboy. "I never stop discovering," he went on evenly. "People read my work and like it!"

She gave him an approving smile. "I'm sure they do. And you shouldn't be offended because I'd never heard of you."

No, he shouldn't. But how easy this would be if she respected him in advance, as so many other women had. If she'd read his previous work and gave him due credit for it.

But nothing was going to be easy with Jeanne Trent. He'd be forced to prove himself from scratch. At a time when he had nothing fresh left to say to his readers or anyone else.

"If it makes you feel any better," she said encouragingly, "my sister Angie has heard of you."

"Wouldn't mind meeting this sister," he said half-teasingly, hoping he didn't sound too eager. "And I know Emmett would like to meet you in spite of everything. He likes the sound of your voice already. Hey, maybe we should get the families together. Sound like fun?"

"Do you think Emmett might remember Toby if he saw him again?" she asked hopefully. "Remember any of his list?"

"No, I asked him and he said there are just too many faces every day."

"Oh."

"But we still could join forces for some holiday cheer. For drinks, or something."

"No," she said dully. "Without a real reason, I don't think it's worth exposing you to the brood at this time."

He stiffened defensively in the maple chair. "Would they disapprove of me?"

"On the contrary! They'd cuff us together, station us under the mistletoe until you cried for mercy."

The very idea brought a grin to his face. "I'm free for dinner."

She chuckled. "When?"

"The rest of my life."

His voice was liquid honey, and the message made her heart to skip a beat. "I'm battling the Potters' protective shield right now," she tried to explain. "Trying so hard to be independent. Despite the fact that Mom brought Toby into Gracie's, they know nothing of what's happened since. For the time being, I'd like to keep it that way. It'll cut down on their interference, and protect Emmett from being unmasked as the rogue Santa."

Ron released a sad sigh. "Okay, if that's the way you want it."

He was so interested. And she was flattered. But just the fact that she was flattered sent hazard signals flashing before her eyes. Real relationships weren't built on a foundation of flirtation and flattery. She was determined to search for something real and lasting again, like she'd had with David. This man traveled all the time, no doubt leaving many interested women by the wayside. She could only wonder how many times a year he affected the right kind of come-on to serve the moment.

Right now he seemed in need of a traditional Christmas, and she just happened to be serving up one.

He was probably the worst kind of choice for a begin-again romance. He'd make his mark and be gone.

If only his brown eyes weren't as tempting as rich, creamy chocolate syrup. If only his mouth hadn't been so hard and kissable under her fingertip.

A smart woman would send him on his way right here and now. If she stalled much longer, Toby would awaken and insist he stay.

She barely recognized her own voice as she offered him another cup of coffee.

5

"HEY, IT'S YOU again. Hi, Ronny!"

Toby burst into the kitchen a short time later, just as exuberant as Jeanne had predicted he'd be. She averted her gaze, hoping Ron wouldn't realize how relieved she was. Toby's presence would keep him here and buy her time to figure out what on earth to do with him.

"Hi, buddy." Ron cheerfully greeted the boy, who was dancing excitedly around the room.

Toby stopped in front of Ron. "Why'd you come back?"

"Well, for one thing, I brought you a present."

The pinball game was an instant hit. Toby plopped down on the floor, and set the game on his legs. "Pitcha! Pitcha!" he shouted, launching a marble-sized baseball into the hollow box. "Can I have a snack, Mommy? Before Fu-Fu comes?"

Ron watched Jeanne move to the cupboard for a plastic glass, then to the refrigerator for a jug of apple juice. "You attached after all?"

"Very funny," she snapped saucily, filling the glass. "Fu-Fu's a pet."

He chuckled. "Could've been a pet name for a frisky friend."

"I'm sure you realize I'm not the kind to give out gooey names like that to even the friskiest!"

Toby climbed onto a chair, and reached for his juice and a handful of cookies. "He is a dog, Ronny," he explained with authority. "A poodle dog."

"Does he come on his own?" Ron asked.

"Fu-Fu brings Eddie," the child replied, stuffing a star-shaped spritz cookie in his small mouth.

"General Edward Chambers is the man with the appointment," Jeanne inserted. "He's an old army man who has his portrait taken biannually with his pooch."

"Sounds like you'll have your hands full," Ron remarked, eyeing the door leading to the hallway.

"But I'm sure Toby would love for you to stay on," Jeanne hastily added. "For a late supper."

He grimaced. She was using the boy as an excuse! She was no better at staking a claim than he was!

"Don't you get it?" the child interrupted, never looking up. "She wants you to sit with me. So I don't run willy-nilly."

Ron pretended to be shocked. "Willy-nilly, eh?"

Toby flopped his blond head once. "Yup."

"Not sure we can be trusted together, Toby," Ron said, struggling to remain earnest. "I mean, we got into trouble yesterday."

Toby grinned toothily. "Yeah, it was all your fault. I told Mommy on you."

Ron chuckled then. "Guess I've caused more than my share of mischief round here. Your mommy probably thinks I need a sitter."

Jeanne was disgusted with herself. Why had she used Toby to bait Ron into hanging around? But Ron wasn't just any man. He'd shaken her up in a crazy, tantalizing way. "Toby usually watches the studio's portable TV," she said with a dismissive wave, giving him a way out. "It's no big deal, Ron, really. We manage."

"It's a big deal to me," the boy objected. "I want to play with Ronny."

"Be glad to stay," he quickly told her.

"Good," Jeanne said with undisguised delight. "We'll have some of my homemade chili afterwards. All I have to do is heat it up." She accidentally grazed him as she passed by. The jostling contact made them both pause for a heart-racing moment. "I, uh, have to get things ready," she murmured. "We won't impose too much, I promise."

Famous last words. Ron hadn't been run so ragged since his last African safari. Not only did he and Toby end up in the studio helping Jeanne properly light the finicky clients, but the general insisted Ron hide beneath the table Fu-Fu was perched upon, and place his larger, stronger hand atop the dog, as though it was Edward's own!

The session dragged on with some background and clothing changes. Ron eventually offered to heat up the chili for a hungry Toby, and begrudgingly served it to order, minus the beans, with exactly three saltines ground into it. Then it was a trip to Toby's bedroom for a pajama roundup, a trip to the bathroom and finally, a bedtime story. Ron was delighted to discover he enjoyed himself every bit as much as the boy.

As Ron tucked Toby in, he couldn't resist quizzing him about his Christmas list.

Toby gasped, scandalized. "It's a secret, 'tween me and Santa."

"But I'm good at keeping secrets."

His lip protruded. "No, Ronny."

"Please."

"Go see Santa at Gracie's with your own grandma."

Ron smiled tightly. Outfoxed by a four-year-old. But rather than risk pushing the child too far, he gave up, and circled the twin mattress to tuck all the edges in snugly.

"Get 'em tight, Ronny. I can fall out."

"Know what you mean," Ron said dryly.

The boy's hazel eyes grew wide. "You fall out too?"

Ron paused, with a far-off grin. Technically, he'd been kicked out on occasion by a tempestuous woman.

"Well, do ya?"

Ron cleared his throat. "Tell you all about it when you're older."

"Tomorrow?"

"We'll see." He moved to the desk where a clown-shaped lamp glowed. "You keep this on all night?" Before Ron could stop him the child had wiggled out of his cocoon, and was flying across the hardwood floor. With small nimble fingers he flicked off the clown's head, and clicked on the lamp's night-light base. As Toby turned, preparing to scamper away, Ron caught him by the shoulder. "Hey, buddy, what's this?"

Toby stared at the envelope Ron had removed from the desk. "My letter to Santa," he said soberly. "Private first-class mail."

"So it is." Ron tried to disguise his delight. What a break! Surely all the things Toby had told Santa at the store were written down here.

Toby leaned against him, yawning hugely. "I drew that stamp for the postman."

Ron's brown eyes shimmered in the dim light. SANTA, NORTH POLE, was written across the front in bold, crooked crayon letters. "So it's ready to mail?"

"Yup."

"Want me to mail it for you?"

Toby bobbed his head eagerly. "Wouldya, please?"

Ron ruffled his hair. "You got a deal! Now, back under the covers."

"Tuck me more."

"With pleasure," he said grandly.

Jeanne was just sitting down with a bowl of chili when Ron wandered into the kitchen minutes later. He had a crafty gleam in his eye that reminded her of Toby when he was up to something.

"Toby settled?"

"I think so." He chuckled. "Are you ever sure?"

"No."

Ron noticed her glass of milk on the counter and brought it to table, then slid into the seat beside her. "Fu-Fu and his master all taken care of?"

Jeanne took a long sip from the glass, giving herself a milk moustache. "Finally! Edward sends his thanks for the use of your hand."

"Hard to imagine that anybody will believe a hand that's younger and nearly twice the right size is really his."

"Perhaps not, but I used a soft-focus lens to buffer the clarity."

"You are a sneak."

Jeanne stirred the steamy chili set before her. "You're a bit of a sneak yourself, Ron. What were you and Toby up to?"

"A little of everything. I have a new and great admiration for parents. I haven't hustled this fast since profiling the rodeo circuit for *Time*."

"Yeah, right. You look like a sleek panther who's just bagged a big one."

He reached out then, and slipped his hand beneath her curtain of hair to make contact with the silken skin at the base of her neck. "And you're a kitten," he crooned. "Caught in the cream." She heard a deep delicious sound in his throat as he leaned across the table and pulled her closer, until he could capture her mouth in his own.

Hot, wet fire. Jeanne's body went limp with longing as his lips grazed hers. His tongue flicked at the ridge of milk beneath her nose. She'd almost forgotten how good a passionate kiss could taste. Almost. A burst of desire buried deep in her belly was rising to the surface and spreading through her with a molten heat.

It had happened with David this way, on their first date in his battered old Mustang. An instant powerful chemical connection. But Ron wasn't like David. He wasn't her type at all! So how could she be letting go this way?

When they finally broke apart and settled back in their chairs, both were a little shaky.

"I should be going," Ron said raggedly, raking a hand through his shag of brown hair.

She gazed at the stove clock to find it was nearly eleven. It had seemed like time had stopped during their kiss, but naturally it was an illusion. A long, fifteen-minute illusion. They'd made out! In fifteen minutes! He'd scraped his chair over beside hers and she'd climbed into his lap!

Ron followed her eyes to the clock and read her thoughts. She was surprised by the passage of time, whereas he'd been achingly aware of each and every second. He'd debated whether he dare palm the underside of her breast over her sweater, or slide his hand beneath it to stroke her back. He'd ultimately done neither, and had broken away when he could no longer control himself.

It had been the right choice, he was sure. This was probably her first intimate encounter since David had died. All in all, he was hopeful and satisfied. He was also fearful and confused. To his delight and dismay, he was falling hard for someone for the first time in ages. A woman he barely knew, had barely touched.

Maybe Christmas miracles could happen to anybody.

They stood up together. Jeanne smoothed her tide of golden hair. "So, you ready to fess up?"

"About what?"

He looked so panic-stricken, she had to laugh. "What you and Toby were up to."

"Tell you tomorrow," he promised.

"You can't mean it!"

"I do believe I have this whole Santa problem licked," he crowed. "If that makes it any easier for you to sleep tonight." Pivoting on his heel, he headed for the front door. She trailed him down the hallway, then moved ahead to block his way.

"I want to know. Right now."

"It's something you should've thought of," he teased, tapping her nose as he reached into the closet for his jacket.

"C'mon, Ron," she coaxed with a hint of irritation. Maybe she was overprotective of Toby, an issue all the Potters agreed upon, but she couldn't abide being left out.

He stepped outside. "Hey, you didn't turn on your Christmas lights."

"It's too late now."

"Oh, please, do it for me."

The words were so natural on his tongue, as though he'd used them over and over again. In bed, out of bed, maybe even under the bed. After a year of just making the bed, she felt a rush of fear and inadequacy. She did her best to conceal it all behind a frown. "Don't know if you deserve the lights when you're being such a difficult fiend."

He descended the stairs, moved halfway down the sidewalk, then waited there with hands clasped. Sighing in resignation, she moved her hand over the switchplate beside the door. The exterior of the house sprang to colorful life. He gave her an enthusiastic thumbs-up, then continued on out to the street.

"Hey, I'm not through with you yet, mister!"

Lord, he hoped not. "You're an incorrigible flirt, Jeanne Trent. 'Night." With a wave, he eased behind the wheel of his rental car.

Jeanne watched his taillights wink into the dark distance, then flicked her lights off in a huff. Outsmarting Toby couldn't have been that easy for him. It simply couldn't have been. He was the incorrigible one, a know-it-all bachelor who needed a good swift kick in the pants. Why, the idea that Toby had told Ron a secret he wouldn't share with her was intolerable, if not impossible! With her chin held high, she marched off toward her son's room for some answers.

"WAITING UP for me, Pop?" Ron entered the apartment thirty minutes later to find Emmett pouring himself a brandy at the portable bar beside his large floor-to-ceiling bookcase.

"No, just took a taxi home from Victoria's." He immediately reached for a second glass, and filled it as well. "We went there after the choir concert, and I didn't want her to brave the roads again."

"Good thinking." Ron eased out of his jacket, accepted the snifter Emmett offered him, then settled into an easy chair.

"Nice seeing Elaine again?"

"Sure was." Ron took a long sip of the strong amber liquor. "Five kids by Tony Rosetti. Wow."

"Could've been you, married and content."

"Tony's not my type."

"Don't be flippant at this hour."

"Okay," Ron relented, laughing. "The same thought passed through my mind. What would've happened if I'd settled here and married Elaine? But I've concluded that I wouldn't have been satisfied, Pop. She said even Tony had been waiting for the chance to fulfill his first dream, and I would've been too. Easier for him to open a garage than it would've been for me to hop a plane for stories."

Emmett's chest heaved beneath his black-velvet dinner jacket. "Ah, then she's but a Ghost of Christmas Past."

Ron affected a shudder. "First you say you're Christmas Future, and now Elaine's Christmas Past. What's my present fate, I wonder."

Emmett's regal face beamed. "If you've begun to wonder, my point is made."

"You should be more concerned with your own affairs," Ron retorted, lifting his lean hip to extract his wallet from a back pocket. He opened the worn leather billfold and extracted an envelope. "I'm still working the damage-control shift for you."

"Thought this was settled, son. No retraction. You had no reason to pursue this matter on my behalf."

Ron was in no hurry to admit he simply couldn't stay away from Jeanne Trent, that he'd opted for some bickering and begging after all. Emmett would crow so loud, he'd wake the entire high-rise. "Well, call it inherent pride, but I couldn't believe there wasn't some simple answer to the Trent family's problem."

"And you claim to have discovered it?" the old man asked loftily.

Ron's mouth crooked triumphantly. "Got hold of Toby Trent's letter to Santa. And presumably the list he whispered in your ear."

"What do you intend to do with it?"

"Steam it open for a look, see if I can't make it right."

"Is it all really worth it, when I can assure you things will work out?"

Ron resisted the urge to suggest that perhaps Emmett should be telling fortunes instead of playing Santa. He turned the envelope over in his hands. "You'd think that Jeanne would've done this herself. But I figure maybe she didn't know about it. In any case, the kid insisted I mail it."

"Sounds like a lucky break."

"Skill and luck." Ron drained his glass with a satisfied sigh. "I feel I'm really getting the hang of this family stuff."

"Really?" Emmett's query was accompanied by an unbecoming snort, but Ron didn't seem to notice.

"Oh, it goes way beyond finding the letter. I took to Toby's routine in a snap—play, dinner, bed." He waved the envelope. "Pull this off, and I'll really be in with Jeanne."

"I'll put the kettle on for a little steam," Emmett announced, heading for the kitchen.

"Why, when you obviously think it's a waste of time?"

The old man paused at the doorway, lifting his snifter in toast. "I don't know how you're going to get skunked, but I can't wait to find out."

JEANNE WAS half expecting the telephone to ring that night. And it did. About one o'clock.

"Why didn't you tell me!"

She sat up a little straighter in bed, and set aside her book. "Now, Ron, you know you didn't give me the chance."

"So you figured it out."

"Yes, a look around Toby's room and I realized."

"I must've come off as an arrogant jackass."

Jeanne tipped her head back against her bank of pillows with a smile. "In a fun, naive way."

"So Toby can't write yet, eh?"

"No, I helped him address the envelope, that's all. He didn't want to show me the inside, and I knew it wouldn't help the cause anyway."

"In case you're wondering, it's bunch of blue squiggles—six in all—with a row of red candy canes at the bottom, along with a big T for Toby."

"You translate those squiggles and the CIA will recruit you for sure."

"Maybe the candy canes mean something," he suggested in desperation.

"Oh, they do—they're kisses. The Potters give candy-cane kisses out at this time of year, and Toby picked it up."

Ron made a soft groaning sound that curled her toes beneath the covers. "You're making those Potters sound mighty inviting. Especially the blond, elfin one with a mean sense of humor."

Her soft laughter rang a little off-key.

"You aren't angry that I took the letter, are you?"

"No. But be sure to mail it, won't you, just as Toby intended?"

"Really, without a stamp?"

"Post offices around the country handle hundreds of them, believe me. And it's only fair to follow through."

"If that's what you want, sure."

"Thanks so much for trying so hard with him, Ron," she said sincerely. "It was very, very nice of you."

"But I haven't succeeded yet."

"I'll think of something." Her tone was formal and distant.

"But I'm committed to helping, Jeanne."

"Surely you've come to realize that I won't be turning Emmett in to Grace Brothers—"

"Well, I did figure—"

"That was more my temper talking than anything. And I'm over it. If there haven't been any other complaints to the manager, I don't want to be the villain who pulls the plug on him."

"Amazingly, as I told you, there hasn't been another one. Aside from the lady at the customer-service counter," he joked. "But I think Lenora's problems with Emmett stem from his off-duty habits."

"Well, anyway, as far as I'm concerned, you and Santa are off the hook. If I could survive this past year with my sanity intact, I can certainly round it off with an answer to this last crisis. Good—"

"Hey, wait! You can't be dumping me! Can you?"

She gasped. This didn't sound like the cocky guy who'd strutted down her walk two hours ago, the guy she'd prepared herself to brush off. This anxious suitor was a lot tougher to deal with. She released a nervous breath. "Oh, Ron. I just don't want to impose."

She was the worst liar he'd ever met! "I thought we were really on to something, Jeanne."

"Is that possible? I mean, we're so different, you and I."

"I'm a man, you're a woman. It's the age-old difference. The most intriguing difference." The sharp intake of breath on the line gave him the same satisfaction. "I should make you kiss me hard and long every time I find out an item on Toby's Christmas list. Presumably we're dealing with six items—"

"As if you can!"

"Kiss you hard and long? You know I can."

How like him to say something like that, to force those intimate memories to the forefront of her mind. As if she needed inducement. She could think of nothing else.

"One thing on the list is something called a Mighty Mite Gas Pump," he announced with pride.

"Are you improvising?" she wondered suspiciously.

"That's a fancy word for lying. But no, Toby let it slip that he'd be getting one soon to gas up his bike and sled." A silence fell over the line. "So it seems like somebody owes somebody a smooch already."

"You were paid in advance."

"And next time?"

"Don't you get the hint?"

Her tone was husky with desperation, but he wasn't going to let her off the hook because of it. He was even more desperate. "Don't try to tell me you're not ready, Jeanne. That kind of bluff would be beneath you."

"No, you're right," she said after a long pause. "I do want to get back in the game. It's you, Ron. The fact that we don't seem particularly compatible. I'm sorry."

"But we hardly know each other!"

"True—"

"So what are you afraid of?"

"Falling for the wrong man, I suppose," she replied honestly.

"How can you know that!"

"I have to think of Toby, too. How disappointed he'd be if it flopped."

"Toby, Toby," he scoffed in disgust. "First you use him to keep me close, now you're using him to dump me!"

"And you didn't use him yourself, trying to get to me by solving his problems?"

"Maybe, but I like him very much. Very much."

"Don't you think you could hurt him, Ron, if you hung around for the holidays, then became bored and disappeared?"

"I wasn't thinking that far ahead." There was surprise in his tone.

"I think way ahead, Ron. I feel I must!"

"Really, Jeanne? Did that policy work for you the first time around?" The angry words poured out and he didn't stop to monitor them. "Do you think your late husband wouldn't give anything to go back and be crazy and impetuous and daring with you? That he wouldn't want you to do the same now if you had a second chance at a relationship?"

"If you were here I'd slap your face so hard your inflated ego would burst like a balloon," she seethed.

"You just don't get it, Jeanne," he attempted to explain. "I haven't taken enough risks myself—"

"A man who's been in most of the world's danger spots?"

"I mean on an intimate level," he confessed. "I've waited way too long to jump into a real kind of relationship. If we could just take the leap together."

"How many times have you used that line?" she snapped.

"Huh?" How could she possibly mistake him for a silver-tongued Romeo, when all he could manage was that single-syllable retort?

"Can't you see I'm struggling? Can't you see I'm having problems coping?" Her voice broke a little. "Even a hustler like you should have the goodwill to back off and pursue other prey. When asked to do so politely."

Politely? He overlooked that inaccuracy. "But we were fine tonight," he said instead. "What happened?"

"I didn't mean for this kind of fight to erupt, really," she admitted in a milder tone. "I've done some thinking since you left and it's clear to me we're all wrong for each other."

"For somebody who'd never heard of me, you sure have drawn some hasty conclusions."

"This wouldn't have gotten so ugly if you'd have just accepted my decision. Goodbye."

The dial tone buzzed in his ear with the ferocity of an angry bee. Ron returned the slimline phone to his nightstand with a frustrated growl. On one hand she'd accused him of being too crass, and on the other she'd been begging him for the understanding of a sensitive male. How could he be both?

He'd never met anyone quite like her. An overprotected mother with the passions of Venus. An overly organized spitfire with the kiss of an angel.

She certainly had a nerve being all those things at once. He punched his pillow and twisted and turned beneath the covers. It would serve her right if he didn't give up, if he forced her to reject him for a saner reason, like disliking his taste in clothes or his snoring. Yes, it would make him feel a whole lot better if she dumped him because he snored too damn loud. All night long. After wild, passionate lovemaking.

Yessiree, being rejected for a good tangible reason like that would make him feel a whole lot better.

6

"SHOULD RUN LIKE a top with these new spark plugs, Jeanne."

Martin Potter's jovial voice echoed through his old high-ceilinged garage, as he closed the hood of his daughter's green Buick the following Sunday. A giant, robust man in his midfifties, with a ruddy complexion and a thick head of straw-colored hair, he was an ideal patriarch in the eyes of his family. Especially to the middle child, Jeanne, presently shivering near the space heater on the workbench. As she stepped forward to hand him a rag to wipe his blackened hands, her pretty face was aglow with hero worship.

"Thanks, Daddy." She had to stand on tiptoe beside the towering, large-boned man to kiss his smudged cheek. "You're my knight in greasy coveralls."

"And you're my princess in denim and flannel," he returned gruffly. "What are you doing skipping around without a coat?"

"Just dashed out to tell you Mom's waiting dinner. Just the kind of Sunday meal you like best. Roast beef and all the trimmings."

Martin lifted a bushy brow. "So the Christmas cards are taken care of?"

"Yes, Toby took your place licking the stamps."

Martin inhaled deeply, unzipped his moss-colored jumpsuit, and peeled it off like a banana skin. "Suddenly I'm starving!"

He shut off the heater and the lights, then angled an arm around Jeanne's shoulders and guided her outside into the snowy twilight and down the narrow backyard path that led to the family's rambling old gray two-story. Jeanne couldn't help noting that, just as Angie had said, the house was plastered with small colored bulbs. Ten times the number on her own place, by conservative estimate. This was supposed to help her and Toby feel more festive?

"The house looks like a movie marquee," she remarked.

Her father pressed a kiss on her flaxen head. "Do you know they make self-adhesive stamps now, baby? You peel 'em off, then stick 'em on. Easy."

"Mom's old-fashioned about her stamps. Said they didn't have self-adhesive angel ones. About these lights—"

"Ah, the hardware store was having a sale, darn near giving them away." He avoided her gaze as he clomped along the slippery walk.

"Sure, Dad."

"Always been a sucker for a sale."

A sucker for his kids was more like it, she silently corrected. Her parents, social workers for the county, had never had extra income to lavish on their children. But she and Angie and Andrew had been loved equally throughout the years and it was the most important kind of wealth Jeanne could imagine. Since her husband's death, however, they'd begun to focus on her and she'd grown to absolutely hate the smothering. How she longed for the old Potter system of democracy.

The old house boasted a small service porch on the back, perfect for storing seasonal clothing and equipment. Martin stopped in the long, narrow room to tug off his boots, leaning against their boxy old freezer for leverage. He expressed surprise to discover Jeanne had lingered alongside him. "Go along into the kitchen, honey," he said. "It isn't more than fifty-five degrees in here."

"Wanted to speak to you, first, Dad. About my life right now."

The crack in her voice set his teeth on edge. He straightened up in his stocking feet, and met her gaze squarely. "If you want to move back in here with Toby, we'd be happy to oblige."

"Oh, Daddy." Her tone insinuated he'd offered her a trip to the moon on the tail of a kite.

"Do anything for you," he blurted out with Potter directness. "Just name it."

"You're doing too much," she said softly. "I appreciate the extra efforts this year. All year long you and Mom have hovered close, paving the way for me. But now, this finale of a million lights and spritz cookies." She rubbed her chilled hands together, undaunted by the fact that he hardly seemed to be listening. "It wasn't necessary. It really, really wasn't."

The big man straightened up, a force to be reckoned with in his rumpled twills and stocking feet. "Can't argue the point."

"You can't?" It wasn't like her father to give in without an argument.

"Nope. Potters aren't known for their subtlety, but we're sharp on the facts, right?"

"Right." She beamed in relief.

"It was a silly waste," he scoffed. "We know that now."

"Now?" she repeated confusedly. "How now?"

He opened the door leading to the kitchen, motioning her ahead. "Now that you got yourself a boyfriend, of course. C'mon, step lively. You'll turn into an icicle standing there with your mouth hanging open."

"I DIDN'T TELL anybody anything and I resent your accusation!" Angie stood erect, hugging their mother's precious china plates at her chest as she glared at her little sister across the dining room table a short time later.

Jeanne shifted from one foot to the other. She'd waited for the chance to speak to Angie alone, then she'd barrelled in here in a fit of white-hot anger to accuse her of nothing less than a felony between sisters—the breaking of a confidence—and was being quickly and efficiently defused. Angie was quite the opposite of the humble blabbermouth caught in the act. "You, ah, didn't?" she spluttered, reaching down to pick up the stack of paper napkins on the crocheted tablecloth.

Angie began to round the rectangular table, slapping down the dishes as if they, too, were paper. "No. Quite frankly, I didn't think anything would come of it."

"Thanks a lot!"

Angie paused impatiently. "Let's face it, sis, at twenty-six, with a son to raise, you'd have to do more than flutter a lash at a celebrity bachelor like Ron Coleman!"

Jeanne's face flamed. "As it happens, he appeared interested enough."

"Oh?"

"Yes," she affirmed with a measure of pride. "And as it happens, I think I'm still a fairly good catch."

Angie chuckled. "Good to hear that you know it. Decide you want to be caught and you'll be on your way."

That was the heart of the matter all right, the process of making the right decision. She intended to approach the dating game with the same kind of care and sense she'd been using to expand her business.

A man like David seemed in order, someone rooted in his hometown, a nut about traditions, an orderly businessman who paid bills well in advance and planned vacations with a set and secure itinerary.

All the things Ron Coleman wasn't.

Ah, but when he'd kissed her, she'd forgotten all about her mental list of qualifications. Forgotten everything, except how she felt. He had the power to coax a woman into blissful submission. But she wasn't foolish enough to believe it was accidental; Ron was a man of experience—another trait foreign to her.

"Hello?" Angie tapped on her head. "Anybody home?"

Jeanne laughed. "I don't blame you for wondering lately. Sorry I accused you. Toby has to be the stool pigeon."

"Naturally. The folks have been pumping him like a well all year long about your activities and emotional state."

"He comes cheap too, doesn't he? A few gumdrops, a can of soda pop, a nose nuzzle from Grandma Cat."

"Since you can trust me—as always," Angie said in a huffy whisper, "give me the scoop!"

Jeanne turned to make sure the swinging door leading to the kitchen was still, then made her way around the table, slipping napkins underneath the silverware. "I haven't seen him since Wednesday."

"That's only four days," her sister pointed out encouragingly.

"It's over, Ange," she whispered adamantly. "Whatever there was, is over."

Suddenly the old oak door behind them creaked. Jeanne tensed as her parents, Angie's husband Brad and Toby filed in, chorusing that it was dinnertime. Martin led with a platter of beef, Catherine followed with vegetables, Brad and Toby trailed after with milk and rolls respectively.

Catherine set her platter on the table and turned to tweak her daughter's cheeks. "There's my crafty girl! Finding a boyfriend all on her own."

Jeanne stared at the slender, misty-eyed woman, still so attractive at twice Jeanne's age. She hadn't seen such raw emotion on Catherine's face since the night of David's accident. "But, Mom, I— He isn't a boyfriend. Not a boyfriend."

Catherine made a clucking sound with her tongue. "Should've told your mother right away."

"Thanks to Toby, we know all about it," Martin chuckled, ruffling the boy's hair affectionately.

"I told ya Ronny's *my* friend!" Toby exclaimed, and pouted when a knowing ripple of laughter filled the air.

"You know, guys, Toby has a point," Jeanne attempted to explain.

Catherine suddenly squeezed her younger daughter fiercely. "We've been so worried. But no more of that nonsense." She released her again. "It's over and you're all right."

Jeanne gasped indignantly. "I have been all right all along. Being a single parent isn't impossible. Millions of women manage it for years."

Her parents exchanged a doubtful look.

"Of course I want to get married again. Someday. To a man as wonderful as David."

"And it's smart to know what you're looking for in advance," Angie said in support of her sister. "No sense wasting time on a fling. Right, Brad?"

The Drillmaster shrugged. "A fling sounds kind of fun."

Jeanne seethed. Couldn't he pick up a simple cue?

"Well it does—*yowee!*" he added, wincing as his wife's heel landed on his suede shoe.

Martin nodded, beaming with his stamp-of-approval smile. "Doesn't hurt to sample all the treats in the window before you buy."

"Daddy!" Jeanne was mortified.

"It doesn't matter whether this Ron is the one," Catherine added sweetly. "We're just thrilled that our wounded duckling's ready to fly again. Finally, we can sleep through the night again. Have a merry Christmas after all!"

A merry Christmas after all? Jeanne's heart dropped clear to her feet in one painful bounce. Their yuletide cheer was in the hands of Ron Coleman? A virtual stranger? A man she'd insulted beyond repair?

They gathered around the table for the meal. Jeanne found it hard to swallow even the soft vegetables. The depth of her parents concern over her solitary life-style really rocked her. Sleep was still lost over it? She surveyed their bright faces, wondering how she'd ever straighten this out.

"So how did you meet a famous man like Ron Coleman?" Catherine asked, leaning over Toby's chair to slice his meat.

"He just rang the doorbell," Toby chirped.

"I met him at Gracie's," Jeanne replied over their amused chuckles.

"Buying me toys?" Toby asked.

"Let's say I was there on your behalf."

"What an odd place to run into a bachelor," Catherine mused. "I imagine the whole thing was a romantic whirlwind. But a man who writes such witty books and articles about exotic places is bound to be adventurous."

"Like a Potter!" they all chorused.

Except for Jeanne, of course. "Surprised you know of him, Mom. You read mysteries mostly."

"Everybody reads Coleman," Martin inserted, jabbing a large potato. "Any sour cream, Cat?"

"No. Use the margarine." Catherine shifted her attention back to her younger daughter, her eyes sparkling. "Why, he wrote a whole book about the way deep-sea fishermen live in the Florida Keys."

Jeanne made a doubtful sound. "Fishermen? You?"

"It's the way he does it, dear," Catherine explained goodhumoredly. "Always gets to the heart of the human condition."

"That was the book right before his report about exploring in the Himalayas," Martin recalled with a chuckle. "You know, Jeanne, those mountains along the border between India and Tibet."

His daughter smiled thinly. "Never been there, but the location rings a bell."

Martin was seemingly unaware of her sarcasm. "He backpacked his way through that range. Ran into some way-out Tibetan sect who took an instant liking to him. Wasn't sure if they wanted to string him up or crown him king!"

The Potters' voices swelled once again, this time in laughter. Jeanne shook her head dazedly. She knew the signs. Ron had been unanimously inducted into the Potter clan—sight unseen!

"He seems nice enough," she ventured carefully, "but he isn't in town for long. Pass the salt, please."

"Where does he live?"

"Uh, Los Angeles."

"With whom is he staying?"

"His grandfather, I believe."

"Where might that be?"

"Como Avenue. Senior high-rise near the lake." For someone who claimed not to be interested, she knew she had too many hard facts on the tip of her tongue.

"And boy, oh, boy, can he play baseball!" Toby announced gleefully.

Jeanne and Angie offered to bring in the dessert and coffee a short time later. Jeanne had baked the tall chocolate cake standing on the counter in the kitchen, so she sliced it while Angie got plates from the cupboard.

"Don't feel bad, Jeanne," she said, setting the dessert dishes on the counter at her sister's elbow. "Playing along was the most merciful route."

"They are pathetically happy, aren't they?"

"Yeah."

"I just didn't know how they felt." She sawed the cake like a lumberjack attacking a mighty oak. "What a dirty trick to spring on me at Christmas."

Angie skimmed her finger through some fudge frosting edging the plate. "Timing isn't their fault, or your fault for that matter. Things just happen. It's fate."

"It's Ron Coleman's fault, pure and simple! And his loony grandfather's."

"Well, you gotta admit, this encounter with him sure beat the heck out of cooing over a half-baked frozen-food fanatic in the supermarket!"

Jeanne turned, a slow and dangerous smile forming on her lips. "Don't you start taking this seriously, too. I need somebody to shed doubt on Ron's potential."

"And if I refuse?"

"I'll tell Brad you failed your dental-hygenist exams the first try."

Angie clapped her hands to her pretty face, mortified. "You wouldn't! You know how picky he is about his work. Why, if he found out, he might never totally trust me again."

"Then play the role that best suits you, the devil's advocate."

As hard as Jeanne tried to steer the after-dinner conversation in other directions, it kept drifting back to Ron.

"Do you have any pictures of him?" Catherine asked. "You always take pictures. Always."

Toby giggled as he licked frosting off his fork. "We got one. Remember, Mommy?"

The child was right. "One did just come from the developers." Jeanne rose, and went to the front hall where she'd left her tote bag. When she returned, she was waving an envelope. She handed it to her father and he edged it open with his large thumb. Everyone popped up and crowded around them.

"Why, this is a picture of the general and his poodle," Martin complained.

Jeanne, standing on his right, leaned over and gestured to the dog. "See that hand on Fu-Fu? That," she told them triumphantly, "is Ron's hand."

Murmurs of interest filled the air.

"What a strong, handsome hand!" Catherine enthused.

Martin studied it. "Doesn't look like he gets a prissy manicure." He glanced at Jeanne for verification.

"No, his cuticles were a bit of a mess." She tapped the photo. "I think the forefinger nail may have even been bitten off."

"An animal!" Angie squealed, forgetting herself. "Wild, virile—no office hours to keep."

For the first time Brad looked a little unsure. "Maybe Jeanne'd better be careful with this guy. Give some thought to her choice."

Jeanne smiled. "I am so sorry my sister stepped on your foot, Brad. It was a mean thing to do." She turned to Angie. "You can't trust some people, that's all there's to it."

7

RON WAS ACCUSTOMED to being sized up at public appearances. Talk shows, college lecture halls, book signings at stores large and small, he'd done them all. He figured that by and large, over the course of time, he'd seen it all.

But this last Thursday before Christmas, settled into Emmett's favorite Grand Avenue bookstore for his only autographing of the season, he seemed to have picked up a new kind of fan club. Or should he say hand club?

His right hand in particular, seemed to interest a bundled-up trio. As he sat at a small square table adjacent to the cash register, putting his signature to books and various clippings bearing his name, he was constantly aware of these people, a middle-aged couple and a woman in her late twenties, who watched his every stroke of the pen. The bookstore, as old as Grand Avenue itself, wasn't very large so customers were in the way if they lingered.

But this small group had the guts to linger unabashedly. Stubbornly planted several feet away from his line of well-wishers beside a display of romance novels, they watched him in wide-eyed wonder.

He tried to put them out of his mind by concentrating on his fans and his grandfather, who was standing beside him to soak up the limelight. Ron was here as a special favor to the old man. The surrounding Grand Avenue shops and cafés were thick with his friends, and he'd promised to deliver his prized grandson to boost revenues and spirits.

Emmett was in his glory at the moment. He'd delivered the hometown hero and intended to reap the rewards with a grand showing. While Ron was dressed in casual khaki, the proud grandpapa was decked out in a tuxedo. While Ron spoke in personal murmurs to his readers, Emmett bellowed platitudes that bounced off the varnished pine walls.

As usual, nothing got by the old fellow, however. As a woman dug through her shopping bag for a clipping she wanted signed, Emmett placed a hand on Ron's solid shoulder and whispered in his ear, "Do you know them, son?"

Ron looked up at him, keeping his expression nonchalant. "Figured they were part of your crowd."

"All bundled up, it's sometimes hard to tell."

"Just hope they're not distant relatives I'm supposed to remember, or old neighbors of my folks."

"Highly unlikely," Emmett assured him. "Though the older lady looks a bit familiar. If only I could place her...."

"She's wearing a wedding band, so I'm sure she didn't make a big impression," Ron retorted under his breath before returning his attention to his task.

The line eventually thinned out, something the trio had apparently been waiting for. They approached the table now. Ron immediately noticed that the younger woman was carrying today's paper under her arm. The store's advertisement announcing his appearance was in plain sight.

"He looks better up close and in the flesh," the older woman proclaimed, eyeing his hand.

Ron swallowed hard. "Excuse me?"

"Can't you guess who I am?" the woman asked. "Who we are?"

Ron's jaw worked as he searched his brain.

"Now, dear," the man chided the lady. "You should pull down your scarf and show your face."

The woman laughed, and playfully complied. That did it for Ron. The combination of the dancing blue eyes, the heart-shaped face, and the blond hair was all too familiar. She was related to Jeanne. All of them were, as a matter of fact. Presumably they were her mother, father and sister.

"The Potters, of course!" he said smoothly. The crazy Potters. Isn't that what Jeanne herself had called them?

"I'm Catherine," the older woman continued. "This is my husband Martin and my elder daughter, Angie."

"Pleased to meet you," Ron said, standing to shake hands with all of them. "I'm assuming you saw the photo of my hand on the poodle."

Catherine gestured to Angie's newspaper. "That's all we had to go on until we saw this appearance advertised in the newspaper. Figured it was about time we saw the rest of you!"

Ron watched them in wonder. They actually made sense. They made staring at his hand for thirty minutes sound reasonable!

"Enjoy reading about your adventures," Martin told him, interest and respect in his features.

"I am the grandfather," Emmett proclaimed heartily, not about to be forgotten for a millisecond.

Introductions were exchanged all around, and Catherine took over the conversation from there. Her eyes sparkled like gems as she surveyed Ron. "It's so nice to finally have more than a hand to go by. The rest of you measures up quite nicely."

Ron shook his head slowly. "I can't get over how much you Potter women look alike." But Catherine was different somehow, not just because of her age. Suddenly he knew. Catherine was happy to see him, genuinely delighted. He could envision just such an expression on Jeanne's sober face, and it made his heart ache. Why couldn't she let go and accept the attraction between them? The rest of the Potters were giving in. He couldn't begin to imagine what they thought or what they wanted, but they were downright delightful about it in any case!

"We felt, under the circumstances," Martin ventured, "that we should get to know each other better."

"Circumstances?" Ron's heavy, dark brows lifted a fraction as he scrambled for equilibrium.

The sister, Angie, who'd been nervously fingering her pale hair till now, interrupted with a hoot. "Now, Ron, you don't have to play dumb for Jeanne's sake."

Dumb? Why, this sister was every bit as irritating as the other, right down to her glum, wary expression. "Meaning?" he queried with a dangerous smile.

"Why, that Jeanne wanted to keep your relationship a secret until you knew each other better!" Angie supplied in a rush. "The jig is up. Toby told the folks everything."

"Oh, I see." He smiled broadly. But his pleasure was short-lived as Emmett cleared his throat. Ron had his own crazy kin to worry about. Mixing them all together might be a sin Jeanne could never forgive.

"So these are the parents of the Jeanne who—"

"Yes, that's right," Ron cut in curtly. "The Jeanne I've been spending time with." He looked from the Potters to Pop. "You really don't know much about our relationship either, Emmett," he said with a cautionary gleam in his eye. "But now that's the cat's out of the bag, I suppose I'll have to fill you in. Later."

"As you say, I suppose." Emmett reared back a fraction, enjoying this new and unexpected game.

"We must have lunch together," Martin announced. "How about right now? My treat."

"You don't have to do that," Ron said politely, though he was curious about this family and, hungry for any information about Jeanne.

"We insist," Martin said.

"Splendid, splendid," Emmett intoned, always one for socializing. "The Café Bon next door serves wonderful salads and sandwiches."

"It's settled then," Catherine said happily, readjusting her scarf. She studied Emmett's face thoughtfully for a moment. "You know there's something about you. I feel we may have met, but I can't imagine where."

Emmett nodded his silver head, giving the matter grave consideration. "I feel it, too...."

"I have some loose ends to take care of here," Ron announced, putting a detaining hold on Emmett's elbow. "Shall we meet over there in ten minutes?" The Potters chorused their affirmation, and filed out of the store with cheery waves.

"Why couldn't I go along with them?" Emmett demanded gruffly, wrenching away from Ron. "The younger one had no man's arm."

"Look, if you don't back off, you could lose that arm of yours. Maybe even your neck."

Emmett's nostrils flared. "Whatever do you mean?"

Ron sighed. "Now that I have all the facts, I can say with certainty that you *have* run into Catherine before."

"Ah, yes, I thought so," Emmett said dreamily. "Following through the first faint glimmers of recognition is such fun. A bonus of mystery to enjoy as one gets older. Where did we meet? In summer stock during the sixties? What did we say to each other? Something sweeter than the most polished script?"

"You were in Grace Brothers a week from last Sunday, telling lies to her grandson," Ron supplied flatly.

"Oh. So she brought the Trent boy in." Emmett sighed wistfully.

"Does it ring any bells, Pop? Any chance you remembering anything the boy wanted?"

"I told you there were too many children to remember anyone in particular," his grandfather said. His features softened as he went on. "This Catherine would've been quite a dish in the sixties, I imagine. I would've liked to have known her then, surely."

Ron rolled his eyes. Emmett was happily married to Grandma Olivia back then, and never would have given this woman or any other a second glance! How could a man so lost in fantasy insist his decisions as Santa were beyond reproach?

"I'm going to ask you one last time, Pop. Will you please reconsider your stand with Toby? Speak to him again?"

"I wish I could be confident that you are sincere when you promise never to broach the subject again," Emmett returned silkily.

"You can!"

"Good, then I can be assured this will be the last time you ask me to compromise my principles and speak to this boy!"

Ron glared at him. "Okay, Pop, okay. But don't miss my point about the lovely Catherine. She's as livid as Jeanne about your stunt. Apparently it took all the Potters and an in-law to keep her from a return visit to the North Pole." Ron shook a finger in his face. "Jeanne somehow convinced Catherine that she would and could take care of the matter—take care of you!"

"How preposterous!"

"For your own protection, Pop, you mustn't let any of them know you're the offending Santa Claus."

"Oh, I think I'm beginning to see," his grandfather said stiffly. "You're uninviting me to lunch."

"As a start, yes!" Ron all but thundered.

Emmett's lined face drooped in disappointment. "But they seem such fun."

"Even if you were to be careful in conversation, Catherine might recognize you at any moment. As it is, we're damn lucky she never got hold of one of your store brochures."

"But you are going to lunch," Emmett pressed. "Jeanne Trent wants nothing to do with you, and still you go to lunch."

"C'mon, Pop. Stay out of this, please."

"I just wonder what you're trying to do."

"I'm not sure myself," Ron hedged, rubbing the back of his neck. "I just can't let go of Jeanne, not yet. Guess I hope that this is a lucky break for me. A chance to approach her from another angle."

"Now was that so hard to admit?" Emmett said in a gentler voice.

Ron stared at his feet. "Yes. I'm not accustomed to being turned down."

"I know. But it happens when we least expect it. When we want things the most. You do really want her, don't you? I mean, you're not pursuing this girl just for the sake of winning?" Emmett asked.

"I wouldn't!"

"It's your nature to chase things the hardest that are just out of reach. Why, you've made a career out of it."

Ron couldn't argue the point. But Jeanne was doing things to his heart and soul that he couldn't begin to explain to his grandfather.

JEANNE WAS IN the midst of scrubbing her kitchen floor when the telephone rang. She slipped on the wet linoleum as she lunged for the wall phone. "Hello."

"Drop everything and get over to the Café Bon."

"Nice to hear your voice, Angie."

"There's no time to waste, Jeanne," her sister hissed.

"Why, they giving something away?"

"You!"

Jeanne frowned, leaning against the handle of her sponge mop. "Have you been drinking?"

"Not yet!" Angie's voice dropped even lower. "I'm on Grand Avenue with Mom and Dad. Grand Avenue, Jeanne."

"I don't mind being left out. It'll give them time to buy me a super Christmas gift."

"This is one gift you don't seem to want!" Angie paused, then her voice rose. "Coming, Mom!"

"Angie—"

"Didn't you see this morning's paper, sis?"

Jeanne chuckled dryly, surveying her damp floor and sink full of scrubbed pots. "Haven't had the time."

"Make the time for the Entertainment section. Page six."

"Why?"

"Not supposed to be telling you at all. Just hurry. Hurry!"

The dial tone buzzed in Jeanne's ear as she stared at the newspaper, still rolled and bound, lying on the table.

"SORRY GRANDFATHER COULDN'T join us," Ron apologized a short while later as he slipped into one of the empty seats at the Potter table. "But he has another appointment he couldn't break."

Their table by the window offered them a clear view of Grand Avenue and Emmett climbing into a taxi with a jaunty wave.

Angie met his eyes then and Ron knew that she was aware of what Emmett did every afternoon.

"Then it seems we didn't need such a large table," Martin declared, looking round the bustling café for the waiter. "Maybe they'd like to switch us to make better use of this space."

"Oh, no," Angie protested. "This view of the avenue, with its decorations, is too pretty to pass up. So easy to be spotted—I mean to spot things from here."

"So what did Brad have to say?" Catherine asked.

Angie regarded her blankly. "When?"

"You just called him, didn't you?"

"I won't be needed at the office until two," Angie said evasively.

"But you knew that already."

"Hmm, so I did."

Catherine gave up on her eldest child, and smiled at Ron over her water glass. "Our cornering you this way may seem strange, I suppose."

"I don't mind," he assured her.

"Good. It's just that, well, Jeanne tires of our interference so we've been trying to accommodate her by doing it behind her back when possible."

His mouth curved politely. "How thoughtful."

"She's delicate right now," Martin explained, his large face pinched in concern. "I'm sure you understand."

"I know about David, of course."

"Tragic, tragic," Martin rumbled. "But it is high time Jeanne got back in circulation. If we seemed a little over-excited about your hand, well, it's because it's the first hand our baby's shown an interest in."

"Nobody could bear to see Jeanne hurt any more," Angie put in. "We just want her and Toby to get through this Christmas with some new and valuable memories to look back on."

"It isn't easy," Catherine said huffily. "She doesn't want our help. And she needs it, with all the problems that keep cropping up to threaten our holiday."

Martin patted his wife's hand. "Now, dear, I told you to forget all about that Santa incident at Gracie's."

Angie took fiendish pleasure in relating the tale to the hapless Ron.

Catherine opened her napkin and slipped it over her lap. "I had only the best intentions when I took Toby there. Who'd ever guess the Santa would go haywire and promise the boy everything he desired?"

"A careless thing to do," Ron said, looking directly at Angie, hoping for mercy. "But I'm sure it will all work out. I've been quizzing Toby myself and have already gotten him to admit he wants a Mighty Mite Gas Pump."

The elder Potters expressed their approval. Only Angie's sour expression did not change. Couldn't she see that he was trying to make up for Emmett's blooper?

"And I intend to question Toby until I find out what all six squiggles on his list stand for," he promised.

The Potters expressed delight over the squiggle revelation. So there were six in all. With the gas pump revealed, that left five more mysteries. Even Angie seemed impressed with his investigation.

"So nice of you to care so much," Catherine said sincerely.

"Glad to do it," Ron assured her. He was beginning to feel more relaxed. "But don't underestimate Jeanne's capabilities. She runs that house and business of hers with amazing skill. There's not a problem she'd shy away from, I'm sure."

Angie nodded, and her eyes slanted to the empty chair. "You can count on it, Ron."

Ron's heart stopped at Angie's cryptic remark. The call Angie had seemed so uncomfortable about wasn't made to her husband, but to her fiesty, temperamental sister. Jeanne was on her way over to take the romantic reins away from her family.

The very idea sent a delicious tingle down his spine. She was going to answer the challenge, after all. Naturally she'd be working against him, trying to prove they were mismatched. But what better way to create some sparks, than with some up-close friction?

THEY WERE EATING their sandwiches when Jeanne burst through the glass door on a gust of chilly air. Ron had never seen her eyes so huge. But it had to be a shock, seeing him cozily ensconced in her family unit.

"Jeanne!" Her parents chorused her name in surprise.

"Hello. Everyone." She sank into the chair originally reserved for Emmett. Ron was captivated by the way her hair lay on her rosy-colored sweater in a soft blond puff, and the way the Angora knit picked up the pink in her cheeks. How refreshing it was to savor the simple things he used to enjoy: a sandwich, laughter over family matters, a pretty girl just in from the cold. It was a much-needed change from being on the run all the time, viewing people and places from a safe, objective distance.

"Angela," Catherine said snappily. "Why didn't you tell us your sister was coming?"

"It's a surprise?" Angie said feebly.

"You don't mind, do you, Mom?" Jeanne challenged.

"Naturally you're welcome," Martin intervened evenly. "Had we known, we could've ordered for you, that's all." He hailed the waitress, who efficiently took Jeanne's order of the broccoli-soup and chicken-sandwich special.

"So you were signing autographs next door, Ron?" Jeanne remarked as she allowed him to ease her jacket off her shoulders and drape it over her chair.

"Yes, this appearance was for Emmett in particular. All his theater cronies hang out around here."

Catherine fluttered her lashes like a teenager. "Isn't that Emmett a dapper man, Jeanne?"

"Quite the character," Jeanne murmured, moving her table setting closer.

"Has Toby met him yet?" her mother pressed. "Oh, how they're bound to get on."

Jeanne opened her mouth to respond, but Ron beat her to it. "Everything's so new still," he pointed out. "We thought it might not be wise to blend the families until we're on more solid ground ourselves." Ron's hopes rose as he glanced at Jeanne's delicate profile. She'd actually brightened a little over the dodge.

"How ridiculous," Martin rumbled. "We expect you and yours for some Christmas cheer. Why, being a bachelor with no home here yourself, we'd simply assumed we'd be joining forces."

"We'll see, Dad," Jeanne said with finality in her tone.

"So where is Toby?" Ron asked, to change the conversation to a safer subject.

"I left him with the next-door neighbor," she said, upturning her cup for the waitress hovering with the coffee pot. "Pass the sugar, Dad?" Knowing the Potters were all watching her sugar intake, she poured two sacks, rather than the usual one into her cup. They wouldn't gain control of everything!

"Toby's playing with that Jason boy?" Catherine beamed with pleasure as she moved the sweetener back out of reach. "How nice."

Jeanne's forehead puckered in doubt, as she stirred her steaming brew. "He is a year older. And in school... He takes advantage of Toby sometimes."

"Toby-boy's sharp like his grandpa," Martin protested. "David was more of a gentle sort, but that Toby can mix it up with the best of 'em."

"And Jason's mother seems very responsible," Catherine added. "I've spoken to her several times over the fence and was very impressed."

"And they won't even be going anyplace by car," Angie blurted out. She clamped her mouth shut again and cringed when it became clear by the disapproving gasps that she'd gone too far.

Jeanne spoke next, in a tone frosty enough to rival the December weather. "I don't care to have all my fears, all my business exposed this way! In—in—front of strangers."

Ron didn't like being called a stranger but he could understand how she felt. He believed she was doing just fine as a single parent, but her family didn't seem to think so. Sure, it was obvious that she was shielding Toby a little too much. But she'd get over it, Ron was certain. Couldn't these Potter people see that their interference was Jeanne's biggest cause for anxiety?

Jeanne simmered beside him, sorely tempted to leap up and announce that charming Emmett was the Santa they so badly wanted to string up, that she and Ron were no couple at all.

That was when Ron played a monstrous trick on her. He reached over, covertly, casually, and grasped her hand under the table. Seconds passed, minutes passed while he held her trembling fingers with a strong and steady pressure. Astonishingly, he'd done the right thing. His touch translated into a quiet, comforting show of support.

There was no denying it, they'd formed a union. Against their mad, web-spinning families. All of a sudden Jeanne found herself part of a couple after all.

But she was not going to admit it. When Ron excused himself to use the rest room in the rear of the café some twenty minutes later, Jeanne followed and was waiting for him by the very pay telephone Angie had used to summon her. She stepped up to block his path in the dim hallway. Ron grinned crookedly and did nothing to avoid the subsequent collision. The angora of her sweater tickled his wrist with a teasing tingle, the tips of her breasts flattened on his chest. How he wanted to put his hands all over her sweater, to envelope himself in her curvy softness.

"How could you let this happen, Ron?"

He eyed her lazily. "Which part?"

"The 'let's have lunch' part! The part that started it all!"

"Oh, no, that's where you're wrong. This deal got brewing the minute the Potters walked into the bookstore for a look at my hand." He snapped his fingers suddenly. "No, that's wrong, too."

"Wrong?" she repeated mutely.

"Right. Wrong."

"Never mind!" She tried to whirl away from him, but he made made a deft grab for her arm.

"Okay, okay. This all started because you showed off that snapshot of Fu-Fu. What a conversation piece, Jeanne. You had to have some motive when you did that." Had she hoped to spur her family into action, to force her to spend time with him against her better judgment? She was obviously getting way too much help from them, but it would be reasonable to suppose that she relied on it to some degree. Families were a blessing and a curse all at once.

"I'm not a snitch as a rule," she said, "but it was Toby who put them on to you. They couldn't believe I hadn't taken any shots of you—"

"Why?"

"Because it's my thing. I take pictures of everyone. Especially in natural poses."

"No wonder you haven't taken my picture. We haven't been in any natural poses yet."

He looked innocent enough, but she couldn't be sure if the innuendo was deliberate. With David, she'd always been sure. She was accustomed to being sure. Why did Ron have to keep pursuing her when he knew he was all wrong in every way!

"I admit I was caught up in the moment, and trapped into trying to please my parents. They wanted to see a photo of you and I happened to have the hand in my purse." He was grinning now, with smug pleasure—as though immensely enjoying her discomfort! "Toby had already told them about your visits," she continued defensively, "and I sort of got caught up in their joyous relief." She threw her hands in the air. "Not only do I have Toby's Christmas to worry about, but the Potters' happiness too. Apparently it rests on whether I have a boyfriend."

"I'm sure they'll get over this obsessive need to meddle in your life," he said consolingly. "And if it makes you feel any better, I agree that they're overdoing it. Everyone mends at different speeds, handles setbacks in different ways. You're doing just fine, Jeanne. And I told them so."

There was that soothing liquid-honey tone of his again, such a nice complement to his comforting handclasp. She suspected it was just a smooth technique, but it still washed over her agitation with amazing effectiveness.

"It's grown worse, when it should be better," she confided. "Whenever I come up for air, they push me under again!"

His brown eyes crinkled with humor. "Just because it's Christmas."

Catherine flew in from the dining area just then, and announced breathlessly, "I just had a brainstorm."

Jeanne smiled tightly. "Take two aspirin and call me in the morning."

Catherine chuckled at her daughter, and absently patted Ron's solid forearm. "I was thinking, dear, why don't I just go around to your house this afternoon and baby-sit Toby. That way you and Ron can spend some time alone, perhaps do some Christmas shopping. That is, if Ron is available." She turned to him then, with a sunny smile.

Ron smiled right back, again wishing he could transfer Catherine's enthusiasm for him to Jeanne. At this moment, Jeanne's expression was strained with thought. She was most likely looking for a way to escape.

"Mother, how do you know I don't have any appointments?"

"Because I took a look at your appointment book yesterday," Catherine fired back matter-of-factly. "So how about it?"

Jeanne wrestled with her annoyance. "Oh, Mom, I don't know. I have my car. Ron must have his."

His lips twitched. Jeanne was a capable photographer, but an alibi-spinner she wasn't. She'd have to come up with a better excuse than that!

"I'll drive your car back. No problem." Catherine looked from her daughter to Ron, waiting for whoops of glee. "Give you a chance to get that gas pump Toby wants."

Jeanne took a breath. "You know about that?"

"Yes, Ron explained how he's trying to wangle Toby's list out of him. Dad and I think he's so clever. Why, we'll have a countdown. Five squiggles to go."

Ron wondered if Jeanne would dare defy her mother. But it was so clear that Catherine was a well-meaning basket case of hope and concern that he doubted it. He wouldn't have dared make the comparison openly, but both women were the same sort of mother, protective, prying and gushing with warmth.

"So, Ron, would you like to make Mom the happiest woman in the world?" Jeanne asked sweetly, sending him a look that begged him to decline.

As if he wanted to take the rap for this imaginary romance going sour. Or miss the opportunity to try to make it the real thing. "Sounds like a great idea to me. We'll shop for Toby, and maybe my parents if you're willing."

With a wave and whirl, Catherine rushed back to the dining room.

Jeanne stomped her boot. "You could've said no."

Ron's handsome face crumpled. "That attitude hurts."

She nodded vehemently. "Good. A little pain will give depth to your performance."

"Then I have the part of the boyfriend?"

She frowned, but there was amusement in her eyes. "For now. But don't let it go to your head. You're the only one who auditioned."

Probably the only one who had guts enough to do so, he thought. Just the same, he truly wanted the part. Ah, Emmett would be so proud when he heard the details of his gig. A starring role in Potter Productions, Unlimited. Live theater at its most challenging. And the payment… Candy-cane kisses were what he had in mind, from his very tempting leading lady.

8

"DESPITE YOUR FAMILY'S obvious problem with snooping, I like them." Ron made the remark as they wandered through Rosedale Mall some forty minutes later. Jeanne hadn't wanted to go to Grace Brothers for the gas pump and he couldn't blame her. Not with Emmett appearing there live and uncensored, doling out dreams to a bunch of wide-eyed innocents like her son.

"I know you're busting with pride because the folks like you," she returned with a saucy lift of her chin. "But don't you think feelings mean a whole lot more when they have substance?"

"What are you driving at?"

"Only that my parents don't really know you, apart from your public image. They have—"

"Haven't gotten close enough to know I'm a self-centered bachelor who doesn't fit in?"

"Mmm, you are in the right business, aren't you? So quick with just the right words."

She wasn't supposed to agree! Anger swelled inside him as they moved along with the flow of shoppers. Never had he tried so hard to please a woman, never had he felt so frustrated. He could hardly believe it.

It was then he thought to look down at her. Why, she was teasing him! The merry twinkle in her vivid blue eyes made her all the more striking. All the more desirable.

"What I was going to say," she began again, "is that, well, my family has no reason to try and palm me off the way they are—"

"You mean you're not a desperate hunter?" It was his turn to tease, and he enjoyed her gasp.

"Haven't you heard a word I've been saying since the moment we met?"

"Of course I have." He curved an arm around her back. "I get the picture, really. Still, I'm glad your family came to check me out. It was my pleasure to meet them. They're genuine and kind and a lot of fun."

She opened her mouth to say more, but he gave her shoulders a squeeze. "Let's just enjoy the moment, Jeanne, and keep our sense of humor. Okay?"

The truth was Ron didn't want any more serious talk. He was afraid she was working her way back to the big brush-off. If he could throw diversions in her path, anything to keep her confused and interested, he was going to do it. Despite her teasing remarks, she really didn't know him well at all. At least not well enough to unceremoniously dump him!

They combed the vast mall in search of the gas pump, and came up empty at toy stores and department stores alike. They did, however find some gifts for Ron's parents, a silk scarf and perfume from Dayton's for his mother and some casual wear from Mervyn's for his father. He'd still wanted a gift his folks could share and show off so Jeanne had steered him to an art gallery, where they'd come upon a limited-edition print by a local artist of Loring Park.

Ron arranged for the print to be framed and delivered to Emmett's. As he dug for his credit card, he noticed that Jeanne, who'd been wandering through the shop, had paused to admire a print of the Como Park Conservatory, a St. Paul landmark boasting a huge variety of plant life in a controlled setting.

He sighed wistfully from his view at the counter. If only she'd smile at him the way she was smiling at that picture. He hastily arranged for the Conservatory print to be delivered to her house, and tipped generously to make certain it would arrive on Christmas Eve. Hopefully, by then, she wouldn't perceive it as some kind of bribe to get her between the sheets. Hopefully, by then, she'd be wearing that smile morning, noon and night!

It was about two-thirty when they left the mall in search of other toy stores. They tried several, but no Mighty Mite Gas Pump could be found. Apparently it was one of the hotter items of the season.

Ron started the car in the parking lot of the last of the bunch, and turned to Jeanne who was rubbing her arms against the winter chill. "I'm so sorry, but—"

"I know! And I know what you're going to say."

"I can't help it!" he squawked.

She waved her gloved hand at the windshield. "Just do it. Get going."

"All right. Next stop, Grace Brothers Toys."

It was close to four o'clock when they entered Gracie's sliding doors with the ever-present customer flow. Ron took hold of her arm, as a burly woman in an artificial fur coat attempted to barge between them.

Jeanne looked harassed. "To think I'd hoped to get Toby's toys on sale. Now, at this late date, it seems I'll be lucky to get them at all, at any price."

"Should've kept that gift certificate," he chided.

She shook her head, still uncomfortable with the idea of such indebtedness. "Emmett's only half-responsible for my fix. He did promise Toby everything. But that darn Toby is to blame as well! Imagine, being coy at that age. If only he'd told me what all those squiggles meant."

"I'll get that list out of him yet," he promised.

"Have to admit I'm warming to that idea." There was a catch in her voice. In this busy store, she felt all the pressures of Christmas, all the pressures of widowhood. She stared at Ron with the huge blues eyes of a lost little girl.

The look pierced his heart clean through. Never had he cared so for a woman. The truth of it washed over him like a tidal wave, making him tremble with fear and desire. At that moment he'd have bought out half the store, done anything possible to put the confident shine back in her eyes.

But storming her with grandstand plays hadn't proven successful, he reminded himself. The only way to win her was with gentle nudges of support. Work his way inside her until she woke up one morning to find him completely indispensable. Suddenly an idea occurred to him. "Go look for the pump," he directed above the merry jingle coming over the public-address system. "Meet me back up here, at the service desk."

"Why?"

"Because I have an idea."

Jeanne mouthed something that might have been "You're crazy," and melded into the crowd.

Crazy like a fox. She'd see.

The line at the service desk wasn't especially long at the moment. Lenora was on duty of course, taking care of customers with brisk efficiency. Despite the static between her and Emmett, he simply couldn't stop imagining them as a couple: The blustery big mouth and the clear head of reason, both with vinegar-dipped tongues. Lenora would be good for Emmett, and there was no question that she already had a thing for him. If only he could make them both see it!

"Next, please."

Ron stepped up to the counter.

"Well, where've you been all day?" Her tone was snappy, and edged with amusement.

"I do have a life outside of Gracie's," he told her airily.

"Yeah, right. What's on the wish list now?"

He made a clucking sound. "You're so sure I want something."

She nodded knowingly. "Decades in customer service have made me a shrewd judge of character."

"Don't think you have Emmett figured out yet," he challenged. "Or do you?"

Her long, thin face flushed prettily. "I'm busy. Extremely, thoroughly and totally engaged."

"Now there's the kind of line Emmett would appreciate." Ron rubbed his belly. "Just speak more from your diaphram, he'd say. Project with force."

She pursed her lips, as though savoring a sweet taste. "If I accused you of shoplifting, you'd be in a spot for a few delicious minutes."

"Okay, Lenora, you're too good for me." He leaned over the counter, bringing his face close to hers. "I'm here to inquire about Emmett's employee discount."

"What!"

His face split with pleasure. "Now, you see, Lenora? See what you can accomplish when you pull that voice out of the depths? Why, you'd be a most convincing Juliet to any man's Romeo."

She planted her hands on the counter, her face resembling an irate mother's. "You're playing Santa again? With this other girl?"

"Sort of."

"How many you got on the string?"

"This one has me on the string," he confessed softly. "I swear, she's the one who counts the most."

Her forehead puckered. "Methuselah know you're pulling this?"

Methuselah, he mused with silent chuckle. How could Emmett disregard this woman's apt wit, her straight-faced delivery? "He doesn't know yet, but he won't mind." His voice grew furtive. "Can I trust you with details?"

"No."

"Okay, okay," he said good-naturedly. "But you wouldn't want that pretty young widow's son to go without a fine Christmas, would you?" Ron could all but see the gears in her head turning. That "a pretty young widow" stuff would surely soften this store veteran, set in her ways.

"But the discount is for the direct benefit of the employee in question," Lenora finally asserted.

"Trust me, Lenora, any purchases that widow would make would benefit Meth—Emmett. He owes this woman for those details that you didn't want to hear about." Her face filled with rage. "No, no, nothing amorous," he hastily added. "This one's my girl. Honestly. Mine, mine, all mine!" Oh, how he loved saying it. Even if he did take a quick and furtive look around to make sure she wasn't close enough to contradict him.

She was visible, struggling with a large box near a teddy-bear display, but certainly not within hearing range.

"Hmm, she was gosh-darn lucky to get that Mighty Mite," Lenora noted.

He didn't dare step out of line to help Jeanne with the bulky box. She gave him a drop-dead glare as they locked gazes, but all he could do was beckon her over.

Suddenly Lenora put a Closed sign out at her station and called for counter assistance. Ron breathed a sigh of relief as a clerk came to handle the line. Lenora was freeing herself to help them out. She held out her arms over the counter, startling the weary-looking Jeanne. "Give the box to me, dear."

"Why?" Jeanne asked testily.

Ron took the box and set it on the counter. "Because," he whispered in Jeanne's ear, "I've wangled you Santa's employee discount."

Jeanne's eyes grew as they rested on Lenora for verification.

Lenora measured her as though looking for some verification herself. "So young to be a widow."

"Yes," Jeanne said bemusedly. "Have the Potters been in to see you about my personal life, too?"

The older woman looked surprised. "What is a Potter?"

"A wild species that could clear this crowd within seconds."

Lenora laughed. "I'd like to meet these Potters one day." Handling the box with strength and dexterity, she set it on the floor and put a large band of green Gracie's tape across the top to verify payment. She then produced a receipt book from beneath the counter. Curling her fingers around her pen she began to fill it out.

"Just accept that Emmett owes you this much," Ron suggested, giving Jeanne's shoulder a pat.

"All right, but I'm paying cash," she said as Ron's hand moved to the back pocket holding his wallet.

"That would work best, with the foggy connection to the employee," Lenora said, pleased. "All I will need is Emmett's signature." She came round the counter, receipt book in hand. "Shall we pay a visit to the North Pole?"

Ron's face lit up like a boy's. "To Santa? Let's go!"

Lenora led the way, blazing a trail down the center aisle. Ron and Jeanne followed a few steps behind. There was a line at the Pole's gingerbread entrance, but that didn't stop Lenora. While her followers paused near the plump photographer, the service clerk kept on moving, her slender form gently jostling people on her way to the throne. Cries of dismay rose. Parents had no quarrel with Lenora's moves, as she was so obviously there for business reasons, but the children viewed her as a low-down line crasher.

"Do something, Ron," Jeanne whispered.

Ron smirked. "Oh, no, those two old-timers are on their own."

Lenora stood at the bottom of Santa's small glittery staircase and the moment a pair of preschool girls bounced off his lap, she handed the pen and receipt book to Emmett. He studied it in confusion.

Suddenly Ron realized that method actor Emmett was in character up there in the big chair and couldn't understand this intrusion. Ron hadn't thought of this glitch. Lenora, her patience about to snap, moved up the first step, making signing motions in the air.

"Get out of there!"

"Take your turn!"

"Line crasher!" All these chants filled the air. Still Emmett sat, blankly staring.

"You silly old coot!" Lenora hissed, as she set a low-heeled pump on the second step. "Sign, sign, sign!"

Suddenly the next second, a chunky boy of about six bounded up behind her and gave Lenora a mighty shove that sent her reeling forward.

"Take your dang turn, lady!" he shouted. "Just hurry up!"

Lenora lost her balance, and her arms flailed in an effort to catch the candy-stripe handrail. It was no use, however. She was a sleek missile, destined for Santa's red-velvet lap. Cries and laughter filled the air as she plopped down on Emmett's thighs, her limbs akimbo.

The old couple looked like animals trapped in headlights on a dark, deserted road.

"That's cute," Jeanne murmured. Ron turned and was surprised to find her standing behind the tripod with a firm grip on the Polaroid camera. To Jeanne, it had been the most natural move on earth. The redheaded photographer had stepped away to help the elves calm the crowd, and Jeanne, anticipating trouble from the angry little boy, had primed herself for the ultimate shot.

The redhead returned, uncertain and harassed. "He'll kill you, Ron."

"No, he won't," he argued with a wink. "Especially when he sees how good he and Lenora are together."

Jeanne expertly took the finished photo from the camera. She showed it to the redhead. "If you just concentrate more, get ready for that smile you know is coming, you get a much more spontaneous shot."

The redhead nodded. "Thanks for the tip. And please keep the picture, my treat."

"IT CERTAINLY WAS NICE of Lenora to sign off on the receipt with her own employee-discount number," Jeanne remarked as they strolled up her walk sometime later. Dusk was closing in and the residential street was alive with colorful lights, including the Trent house.

Ron was moving slowly, reluctant to let their date end. "I'm sure she wishes she'd thought of it in the first place."

"Does this mean my discount days are over? I mean, Emmett looked furious. He even refused your ride home."

"Don't you worry. Once I get Emmett's feet soaking tonight, I'm going to strike some kind of deal with him for the unlimited use of his number."

Jeanne skipped up the snow-dusted steps, and turned to face him with shining eyes. He'd crowded in close but she didn't seem to mind. "I doubt we'll ever be allowed back in that place, though. The manager, Bickel, was beside himself."

Ron lifted his broad shoulders beneath his leather jacket. "Thank goodness Lenora managed to calm him down. She certainly went to bat for Emmett. And then when he scooped her up in his arms near the candy machine for that grand kiss... Wow."

"Wow is right. I simply assumed they were already a hot item," Jeanne admitted. "Don't see that kind of chemical explosion very often."

"Don't you?" His voice was a husky croon as he cupped his hand under her chin.

Jeanne trembled as he tipped her face to his. He smiled gently, feeling the vibration. "You're quivering in your boots."

"Guess the whole scene just got to me," she offered weakly. "I do believe this kind of thing could become addictive."

He smiled wolfishly. How could he help it, huddled so close to the sexiest woman ever to wear a hood! "Care to tell me what you mean? Exactly?"

"Why, the employee discount, of course! That glorious twenty-percent reduction lopped right off the top."

He chuckled dryly over her feigned innocence. "Torturing me must be at the top of your wish list this year."

She made an airy gesture with her gloved hand. "Someplace near the top."

"What would you have done if we hadn't met?" He posed the question teasingly, but was really quite serious about the answer. He would undoubtedly be dwelling on Christmases both present and future well into the night and didn't want to be the only one losing sleep.

She didn't reply, however. But by the distress and delight on her delicate features, he figured the odds were good that she would indeed think about his question.

"All teasing aside, Ron," she eventually said, "I do want to thank you for the adventure today. What I thought was going to be a grim mission turned out to be delightful. And so successful."

"I think you'd rest easier if you looked upon Toby's mystery list as some kind of scavenger hunt. I know I do. I haven't had this much fun at Christmas in years. And for that, I want to thank you."

And words weren't going to be enough for him, she realized, her pulse jumping to life. The glitter in his brown eyes flashed the message that he wanted to kiss her.

Jeanne could feel the knob of the storm door pressing into her spine as she leaned back. She could easily slip inside the house, but then her eyes dropped to his mouth. It was curving seductively, reminding her of their last long, searing kiss. She could still get away, she knew. Until she licked her lips.

At that point it was too late. His mouth was on hers in a flash, with a hard, steady pressure.

It was as good as the last time. Jeanne could feel her knees giving way. But Ron was right there to catch her, to snare her in his arms and tug her as close as their jackets would allow.

"You owed me that," he murmured into her hair.

"How so?"

"It's all part of the scavenger hunt." He stroked her cheek with his gloved finger. "One gift revealed, one candy-cane kiss delivered."

"What!"

"Remember for every item I discover on Toby's list, I get a Potter candy-cane kiss."

She rocked back on her heels, and sized him up in the twinkling light. "Seems there are a lot of rules to this game of yours."

"You make finding kissing excuses tough on a guy," he complained. "Do you realize there isn't a single sprig of mistletoe in your entire house?"

"Yes, sure, I know." He'd actually looked for the stuff. For the excuse. She was flustered and flattered and confused. And she wanted to get away from him, to think. She anxiously tried to wiggle away from the doorknob, but he leaned closer and slid his arm over her head, bracing himself with his palm on the door. "What do you think you're doing now, you—"

"I'm making a good show for your mother," he calmly interrupted. "She and your son have their noses pressed to the window on your right."

A moan escaped from her as she resisted the urge to turn for a peek. "Oh, no! The Potter push again."

"Must say I'm taking a shine to that push."

A flicker of the old fire flashed in her eyes. "Depends how a Potter uses it, Ron."

"So show me how it's done right." Grasping her slender face firmly in his free hand, he kissed her again, deeply, passionately, desperately.

Her long, pale lashes fluttered in surrender. The only heat in the whole ice-cold universe suddenly seemed centered in their hot, wet kiss. The fact that it was a show for her mother should've taken the edge off it. But it didn't. She couldn't think beyond Ron and the dormant longings he was awakening inside her. The way his masculine scent made her think of uncomplicated sex.

He released her then, and she sagged against the door frame. Deprived of his heat she was lost. Chilly and lonely, too.

Just as she was working up the energy to flounce into the house, Catherine popped out, like a champagne cork from an extra-lively vintage. She was attempting to look exasperated, but the glee in her faintly lined face was unmistakable.

"Don't forget I have a husband to feed tonight," she greeted them, shivering inside her bulky cable-knit sweater.

"Ron was just leaving."

"He doesn't have to!"

Jeanne was mortified. "Mother! I think I can handle this goodbye without you."

Catherine's face remained cheery. "So did you find the toy?"

"We did," Ron told her with a measure of pride. "Even got a dis—"

"A discount from a woman at the service desk," Jeanne cut in, wanting to make certain that Ron didn't slip and mention that Emmett, the offending Santa, was on hand at the store.

Ron took the hint. "She's a dear old thing, a friend of my grandfather's."

"How that man gets around," Catherine marveled. It was obvious she found the trait a charming one.

"He's smooth," Ron said, not quite up to matching her enthusiasm.

"Did Toby have a good time next door?" Jeanne asked.

Catherine rubbed her bare hands together. "He certainly did. As a matter of fact, he brought Jason along and they played in Toby's room for the longest time. And you'll never guess what happened."

"Mother, don't make me guess," Jeanne chided. "Not about Toby."

"But it's good news, dear. You see, I was passing by the bedroom and heard the boys talking. When I realized they were discussing Santa I paused to listen."

"Oh, Mother!"

"Well, we need that list, don't we?"

"I hope you didn't stand there thirty minutes, prying into their business."

"Barely twenty," Catherine assured her.

Jeanne inhaled sharply, then noticed Ron's twinkling eyes. There was humor in the situation, she realized. And it wouldn't hurt her blood pressure to remember that.

"Did you find out anything?" Ron asked the older woman, who was clearly about to burst with excitement.

Catherine made an X in the air. "We can cross off squiggle number two. Toby is expecting a remote-control car!"

"A what?" Jeanne all but shrieked.

"They make them for preschoolers," Catherine said soothingly.

"But they run those things in the street!"

"Not necessarily," Ron said gently. "You can take him to a park, or parking lot."

Catherine squeezed his arm. "I was going to pick one up someplace, but if you have a discount at Gracie's..."

"I'll be glad to take care of it," Ron offered. "The pump is still in my trunk.... Hey, why don't I keep Toby's stuff at Emmett's place, until we can get it all collected."

"Use your place as Santa Central, you mean?" Jeanne asked.

"Sure, why not?" Ron pretended to mull it over, as though the idea was brand-new and spontaneous rather than hours old and contrived. He hadn't brought it up earlier because he'd expected to be turned down flat. But that wouldn't happen now. Catherine wouldn't let it.

As expected she nodded vigorously. "Considering that Ron's committed—"

"Mother, really! Committed?"

Catherine looked a bit sheepish. "Can you deny it? Not only is he on the trail of the list, but he's going to make the buys through Gracie's."

"But—"

Catherine forged on. "And I must warn you that Jason is already searching his own house for gifts. It may be impossible to stop Toby from following suit."

"Well, if he proves to be a snoop, we certainly can't blame a neighbor for it, can we?" Jeanne retorted. "Not with his heritage."

Catherine folded her arms indignantly. "I hope you're not implying anything."

"I'll even wrap them," Ron broke in to promise. "Tie them up in neat ribbons."

Catherine beamed again. "Ah, so sweet."

"Ah, the ties that bind." Jeanne added, with less exuberance. She'd always been in charge of Toby's things. She certainly hadn't intended to entrust Toby's Christmas presents to Ron. In a way, it seemed riskier even than lovemaking.

Now where had that idea come from? she wondered. Why, he wasn't even kissing her.

The door creaked open and Toby popped out of the house in jeans and a sweatshirt. "Hey, I wanna have some fun too." He tipped his face up to survey the adults. "What's goin' on?"

Ron ruffled his blond hair. "Nothing at all."

Toby squeezed his fingers. "C'mon inside, Ronny. Let's play."

"I can't tonight. I have some writing to do."

Catherine clucked in regret. "I thought you were on vacation!"

"Well, I'm doing an article for the Minneapolis *Clarion*. Hometown boy angle," he explained. He gave Jeanne's nose a playful tap. "But don't worry, our special deadline is my first priority. 'Night everyone."

Jeanne herded her family inside, determined that they not all stand on the stoop, waving farewell like a bunch of dopes. Catherine left soon after, blissfully convinced that Jeanne was on the road to an exciting romance.

Jeanne attempted to push all such thoughts out of her mind as she went about the business of making a hamburger hot dish. She found herself twitching her nose like a bunny's, however, over and over again in an effort to shake off the tingle his tap had left behind. In spite of her best efforts, she couldn't stop wondering just what it would be like to be really touched by him. All over...

She reached for her frying pan, then slammed the cupboard door. How dare he do this to her! Tempt her when she'd made it all so clear— She stopped herself abruptly. Clear as mud. That's what her message was like. She melted into his kisses, kissed him right back. And when he pressed her body to his, did she stiffen or wrench free? Oh, no, she turned into a soft pliable Raggedy Ann doll.

But it was all his fault just the same. If he weren't so sexy, so handsome, so strong all the time, she wouldn't be so attracted to him.

It simply wasn't fair. He was all wrong for her and had no business trying to convince her otherwise. How dare he act so irresistible when he was so obviously unsuitable?

9

RON WAS BUSY pounding the keys of his laptop when Emmett arrived home about ten. He couldn't see the front door from the dinette table, but he was quickly alerted to the fact that his grandfather wasn't alone. He listened intently for a moment, then relaxed again. It was Lenora's soprano blending with Emmett's rich bass. Soon they appeared in the room, minus their coats.

"Oh. Ron. You're here."

Emmett's greeting was flat, but Ron wouldn't give him the satisfaction of noticing. Instead he feigned raw terror. "Grandfather, Lenora. Together! If you two have joined forces, what chance do the rest of us have?"

Lenora shook a finger at him. "As if this isn't what you wanted in the first place!"

Ron grinned. "Okay, I confess. But you can't blame a guy for wanting to ensure his Gracie's discount."

"We'll help with the widow's boy, won't we, Santa?" Lenora lifted her chin as she regarded the grumpy Emmett.

"A grandson should use his own kin's discount! Not a lady's! Even if the lady is splendid in every way," he added silkily.

Ron rolled his eyes. Emmett's Romeo, as usual, was way over the top. "But you forced me to turn to another, Pop."

"That wasn't your Pop. It was Santa Claus, busy with his job."

"Well, I'll give you another chance tomorrow. We need a remote-control car. Suitable for preschoolers."

"If he doesn't make the purchase, I'll come through again," Lenora promised.

"I'll do it. Out of costume, before curtain time, as it should be." Emmett took special interest in the fact that Ron was typing. "Working on that article for the *Clarion*?" He turned proudly to Lenora. "Ron's snagged a job, doing an article for the paper across the river."

Ron rolled his eyes. "I never feel unemployed, you know that. All in all, I work more hours a year than most."

"Just like to tell people you're working, is all."

In truth, Ron hadn't even started the article until tonight, he'd been so wrapped up in writing about his experiences with the Trents. Writing about Jeanne and her family had helped him clear his head and put the situation in perspective. The people in his trade always said it was the cheapest form of therapy. And Ron agreed.

Emmett stalked to the table, clutching a stack of mail. Ron saved his work and cleared the screen. The old man was too wound up in himself to notice the bid for privacy.

"I stopped by the box downstairs. Something for you."

Ron held out his hand, but Emmett slapped the square green envelope on the table instead.

"There! How do you like having the unexpected thrown at you?"

"Not fair, Pop," Ron replied calmly. "I throw a whole girl at you, and all I get is this crummy card." He studied the return address. "Hmm, from the old neighborhood." Emmett handed him a letter opener, then came around to spy over his shoulder. "It's a party invitation. Sleigh ride up at the apple orchard, just like back in school."

"That Elaine was always a nice child." Emmett turned to Lenora. "She's the one you presented the gift certificate to last week."

Lenora smiled. "Seemed very nice."

"Yes, Ron could be settled with her, you know, but he dumped her after graduation." Emmett set his hand on

Ron's collarbone. "Wonder what she wants with you now? To show you she's done all right, maybe?"

"Most likely," Ron conceded, remembering how uncomfortable she'd been, caught looking anything but glamorous.

"Well, from a feminine perspective, I feel you owe her the chance to show off a little," Lenora observed. "It's no fun to be dumped at any age."

Ron objected. "I didn't mean to hurt her. Don't know if I even did."

"It'd be a proper closure to Christmas past," Emmett recommended.

Ron twisted in his chair, his temper rising. "I'll decide if I'm going."

"Take that widow along," Lenora suggested with brisk practicality. "Then everybody can impress everybody and part friends."

Or more than friends, perhaps. How nice it would be to get Jeanne away from the pressures of Christmas and her family. Maybe it would advance their relationship beyond Santa and scribbles. Ron nodded, smiling at Lenora. "I really like this one, Pop. Don't you let her slip away!"

Lenora scoffed. "I'm no passing fancy to any man, no matter how dynamic he may be!"

Emmett shook a fist. "Don't start with that Casanova stuff again."

"You promised me sherry, old-timer. Don't offer me any of those sickening wine coolers!"

"Wouldn't have the things under my roof!" the elegant actor thundered.

Lenora glanced at her watch. "It's a work night, you know. If you don't get moving, you won't have me under your roof, either. Or in your lap again."

Emmett frowned as he rummaged through his liquor cabinet like a common thief in the night. "Where is the blasted sherry, Ron?"

"In the kitchen. We used it in that cherry dessert thing, remember?" Taking up his notes and computer, Ron quickly headed for his bedroom.

"A SLEIGH RIDE this Friday night? Two days away?" Jeanne moved around her studio the following morning, her cordless telephone tucked under her chin. "Of course I sound breathless, Ron. I have a boy shoveling in cereal and a church choir coming for a portrait!"

"Can you keep Toby occupied without me?"

Jeanne smiled faintly at his interest. He really did seem to like being in the thick of their ordinary life. Crazy, but sweet. "We'll manage." She took some film out of a wall cupboard, set it on a table near her tripod, and examined the box to make sure it was the right speed. "Just have to keep him in view. So why is this date so last-minute?"

"You're not an afterthought, if that's what you think."

She fell silent. That was what she'd figured. How many afterthought invitations had she received this past year? Oh, yes, let's invite the poor widow. Or let's not. How many times had she been overlooked? Oh, how anxious she was to get to the end of this awkward year of firsts!

He swiftly went on. "I just got the invitation yesterday. A bunch of my old school pals get together every year for a sleigh ride. We've been doing it since the tenth grade."

"Oh, I see." She felt better, and it showed in her tone.

"I'm rarely in town, but I happened to run into my old girlfriend—happily married with five children, by the way—and she must've thought of me for that reason."

"How'd she look? The old girlfriend, I mean?"

"Happy. Can I please come over!"

"Wish you wouldn't."

"But why, Jeanne?"

"Just a minute." Jeanne hurried to the studio door and closed it firmly. "Listen, I have another mission for you. If you're interested."

"Oh?"

"Don't make that sound."

"What sound?"

"That purry growl."

"Didn't know I was."

"Liar." Her own voice was a growl now but more threatening.

His chuckle rippled over the wire. "Okay, tell me what you want."

"I've uncovered another of the scribbles," she confided happily.

"Good for you! What is it?"

"A basketball."

"That's an easy one. I'll get on it today, along with the remote-control car."

She took a hesitant breath. "You don't mind, do you?"

"Give me my candy-cane kisses in return and we'll be square."

Her laugh was merry and spontaneous.

"You know, Jeanne," he said with sudden inspiration, "I bet we can guess the next scribble as well."

"How so?"

"Well, don't you think Toby would expect a hoop with that basketball?"

"You know, he would," she agreed. "He's wanted one since last summer."

"Great. I'll add it to the shopping list."

She sank into the chair at her cluttered desk, a deep sound of relief rising from her throat. "I know I seem a wreck about all this, Ron, but every scribble we decode, well..."

"I understand, honey," he said gently. "It decreases the odds that Toby made a wish that had something to do with his father."

She blinked her moist eyes. "Yes, exactly."

"We're almost there. Four wishes down, two to go."

"You've been wonderful about everything," she said with a sniff.

"Wonderful enough to get a real date out of you?"

She made a doubtful sound. "Meeting your old girlfriend?"

"And my other long-lost friends."

"I'm surprised you don't want to dazzle the old crowd with some knockout. A foreign correspondent, a Miss America."

"It's probably what they would expect—"

"See!"

"And maybe a few years ago I might have done it, just to show the guys." He sighed heavily, then spoke as though dredging up his words from the depths of his being. "But I've come full circle, Jeanne. I started out with an angel of a girl and I'm back on track again. With you."

Damn him for saying the right thing! Jeanne tipped back in the springy chair, and rubbed her temples, then the lips he'd kissed so long and so well. She had, of course, imagined dating him for real. It fit right in with making out in her kitchen and dining with her family. Why, most people would have started right off with a date or two before all the rest.

But to start off with his old crowd? That would be a tough, bonded audience full of preconceived notions and expectations. No way would they mistake her for some sophisticated global player. Oh, how she'd love to pass on this one. But he wouldn't want to go alone. If she said no, she'd run the risk of losing him to another date. The idea of losing him to someone else sent a painful jab clear though her. Despite all her precautions, she was growing more and more attached.

"Jeanne?"

"I'm thinking," she claimed nervously.

"I know you must have reservations," he pressed on. "I expected it."

"Oh, really?" she challenged in a sharper tone.

"You'll perhaps be the only stranger," he went on evenly. "Won't know the inside stuff. And then there'll be the curiosity to face, the questions about your life."

His insight gave her the strength to play devil's advocate to her own fears. "I'm sure everyone would be most friendly."

"I can guarantee that much."

"And there won't be questions I haven't answered before."

"So true."

"And we won't have to tell any lies together, for the first time."

His rich laughter filled the wire. "Now who's selling whom?"

"Okay, Ron," she decided abruptly. "It's a date."

There was joy and surprise in his tone. "Great. Don't know what tipped the scales—"

"That's easy," she cut in saucily. "I see my chance to be needed by you for a change." Without giving him the chance to respond, she slid her finger over the Disconnect button.

IN ALL HIS LIFE he'd never understand women. When Ron stabbed the Trent doorbell on Friday shortly after four, he should have been the happiest man alive, but instead he was angry.

More than ever, he was sure that Jeanne was the woman for him, but he couldn't help but wonder if he was getting through to her at all. Could she truly be blind to the fact that he needed her? This was much more than a game to him, a scavenger hunt over a Christmas list. Did she really think he'd go to all this trouble just for a little holiday fling?

He most certainly wouldn't. And she should know better by now!

Was he somehow at fault for her nagging misconceptions? He shifted from one boot to another and adjusted his new royal-blue ski jacket, self-recrimination oozing over his flaming temper like extinguishing foam. Maybe he hadn't made his stand clear enough in his effort not to push her. Maybe he was still coming off like one of his press releases: reckless, tough, larger than life.

She opened the door then, hopelessly pretty and fragile in a bulky, red-nylon ski suit. "Sorry to keep you waiting."

He stared at her mutely. At that moment, every setback they'd shared was melted to nothing by her wide and lovely smile. She looked nothing short of a dream date just then, nervous, breathless and ardent. At twenty-six she could easily pass for an impatient teenager.

What was he angry about? For the life of him he couldn't remember. He walked Jeanne toward the car feeling more than a little like an eager teenager, himself.

"Where are we headed?" Jeanne asked as she clicked her seat belt into place.

"East to Marlowe, a small town near the Wisconsin border." Ron made the reply as he backed the rental car down her narrow driveway with a little more speed than was wise. He couldn't help but notice she was staring at her neighbor's house, the white stucco one where Toby would be spending the evening with his pal Jason. He hoped she'd be able to leave family concerns behind, that they'd be able to forge a new path as a couple.

"Elaine's Uncle Chet has an apple orchard up there," he continued. "He runs sleighs through his property at this time of year to supplement his income."

Jeanne studied his profile. "So, Elaine must be the one? Your high-school flame?"

He gave her a surprised look as he slowed for a stop sign. "Yes, how did you know?"

"Your tone, that's all."

"It was all over long ago," he assured her.

She reached over and patted his thigh. "I'm sure it was, Ron. All I mean is, because I married my school sweetheart myself, I know just how you must feel. I'm touched that you're still fond of her."

Ron shook his head in wonder. A woman who understood him. It seemed almost too good to be true.

LITTLE HAD CHANGED in Marlowe. Ron remembered the general location of the orchard and with the help of some road signs, and easily rediscovered the long private road leading to Chet's old, rambling farmhouse and barn.

There already were several cars parked in the small roped-off lot near the barn. Ron came to a stop there. Jeanne didn't get out in the open spaces much and popped out of the car with enthusiasm.

"It's right out of a Christmas card, Ron!"

He rounded the car and curved an arm around her red-suited shoulders. She hugged his waist, and together they marveled over the landscape. Dusk was setting in fast and the moon was illuminating the snow on the ground. Rows and rows of small trees lined the property, their branches heavy with tiny white lights.

There was activity near the barn, so they slowly strolled in that direction. Once they cleared the house they had a clearer view of what was going on. Two dark Morgans were harnessed to a large black antique sleigh. A group of joyous adults, six in number, were clustered nearby around a small bonfire.

Ron called out to them.

Hoots and hollers followed, and many expressions of shock over his appearance. Ron took all the teasing like a good sport and introduced Jeanne at every turn.

When all the hugs and handshakes had been exchanged Jeanne stood at his elbow, digging her toe into the mix of snow and dirt, feeling awkward. As was common with old friends, the men and women had divided, forming separate groups on either side of the fire.

Jeanne was unsure what to do. Her dating skills were dead. That was all there was to it. From the frozen-food section in the supermarket to the vast frozen tundra was too broad a jump to make so soon.

"Jeanne, is it?"

Jeanne turned to find Elaine squeezing her elbow. "Yes."

"Come join the girls," she invited in a merry whisper. "We want to hear all Ron's secrets, the ones his folks don't know or won't tell us."

"Hey, Laine!" Ron made the mock protest, but was relieved. Jeanne knew nothing particularly juicy about him to share and in his opinion she needed the female companionship.

Before Jeanne knew what was happening, she'd downed two hot-rum drinks and was telling everyone about the time she and her friends traveled to a fair not far from here in Wisconsin to get an interview and photos of the Beach Boys for their school newspaper. The story, which involved the police and local radio station, gradually caught the attention of the men, who in turn edged their way around the fire to listen.

"And that was the inspiration for Jeanne's chosen career," Ron proclaimed, tugging her close.

Hoots and laughter followed.

Elaine's Uncle Chet made his way down the lane from the house, announcing that it was time to climb aboard the sleigh. The men and women paired off, adjusting each other's mittens and caps.

Ron removed his glove for a moment to tap Jeanne's nose. "Having fun?"

Jeanne giggled, her face flushed by the chilly air and alcohol. "There's that purry growl again. And yes, I am. I'd forgotten how nice it is to let go and mingle this way. A lot of our old friends, David's and mine I mean, sort of drifted out of my life this year." She shrugged beneath her bulky clothing. "Guess they didn't know what to do with me."

Ron didn't even know them and still found himself angry.

She easily read his frown. "Can't blame them, really. I wasn't ready to date, and was the odd person out at a dinner party."

Ron found this strict social code surprising, but he responded lightly. "All those women were probably afraid you'd attract their husbands."

She laughed and rapped his chest with her mitten. "You obviously mingle in a whole different way."

"We'll just have to experiment and see."

"Hey, c'mon, Ron!"

He turned toward the sleigh. Everyone was crowded together on the cushions. Chet gestured to a spot big enough for one. A perfect fit for the two of them. With a grand sweeping gesture he scooped Jeanne into his arms and climbed aboard.

The powerful horses trotted along the snowy paths between the rows of lit-up trees at a brisk tilt. The wind was pretty nippy, but Elaine's husband Tony started a round of Christmas carols to warm things up. Everyone joined in, frequently botching the words of the famous songs.

All the while Ron held Jeanne in his lap. Under other circumstances she might have been uncomfortable with the way he was nuzzling her neck and pressing his hands into her belly. But in this crowd of people who'd been married for eons the atmosphere was casual, and very affectionate. Did she dare begin to think about rebuilding that kind of relationship so soon? Had she been so fortunate as to find someone right all over again without a lengthy search? Only time would tell. All she knew for sure was that it felt so incredibly good to belong to someone again. To let go and have some fun.

A huge buffet dinner followed in the farmhouse kitchen. Elaine's Uncle Chet and Aunt Doreen followed their guests round the main floor of the house offering food and pitchers of hot-rum drink. The hours slipped by in a glorious blur of singing, talking and smooching under the mistletoe.

Ron was sitting on the large rust-colored sofa with Jeanne when it occurred to him that he should hunt up Elaine. "Naturally, everybody chips in for this extravaganza," he murmured to Jeanne before rising on unsteady legs. Jeanne blinked dizzily as he cornered his old girlfriend near the dining room.

There was nothing to worry about, she told herself sternly. Elaine was a happily married woman. Still, Jeanne couldn't help but envy the easy body language between them, the way Ron pinched her chin. It was the same way he pinched *her* chin!

"Ah, Jeanne."

Jeanne slowly turned to find that Cathy, a tall brunette married to a plastic surgeon, was sitting down on the cushion beside her. Cathy was definitely the most monied of the bunch. Jeanne's plaid blouse and black slacks probably cost less than the woman's silver headband.

"You look like you're in a daze," Cathy observed with good humor.

"Not used to drinking so much," Jeanne admitted, tipping her glass mug in a toast. "And I've just been admiring the Christmas tree in the corner," she thought to add. It was on Ron and Elaine's left, a perfect cover for spying on them.

"Yeah, must be nice to have so many ornaments. Different kinds with memories attached." Cathy sighed wistfully. "Doug and I have gold bells all over the tree. He likes things orderly, you see."

"Some people do," Jeanne said absently. Ron was squeezing Elaine's shoulders now, digging his fingers into her inexpensive pink-and-white sweater. What were they saying to each other? She turned back to Cathy with searching eyes. How could Elaine look far more stunning in her discount-store sweater than Cathy did in her elegant, melon-colored cashmere pantsuit?

"Ron says you have a son," Cathy prompted.

"Yes, Toby." Jeanne's expression softened as she gave the woman her full attention. "He's four."

"I have a four-year-old girl," Cathy told her. "We really should get the children together."

"That would be nice."

"I don't live all that far from you. In North Oaks."

Jeanne smiled. Everyone in town knew of the elite community. "Sounds wonderful. We'll arrange something after the holidays." She stood up. So did Cathy.

Cathy reached into her small handbag. "Here's one of my cards. I'm a realtor by trade. You can reach me at home or at work."

"Sounds wonderful." Jeanne struggled to keep her features even, though the mission to disrupt Ron's rendezvous was eating at her like a fever. "Now, I believe I'll just go have a closer look at some of those fine old flames—I mean ornaments." She patted Cathy's arm. "Excuse me."

Jeanne was disappointed when she swiveled around, however. Ron was nowhere in sight. And neither was Elaine.

With as much indifference as she could muster, Jeanne paused by the tree to examine its treasures. She peered through the doorway into the dining room to find that most of the guests, including Tony, were in the middle of a boisterous round of poker. But Ron and Elaine were not in sight. It took all her self-control to stay in place for several seconds, admiring a hand-painted angel on a loop of gold lamé.

Was Elaine the one he still wanted? It was unlikely that he could have her ever again, Jeanne speculated. She and Tony seemed hopelessly in love. And Elaine's Uncle Chet had proudly shown her the framed photographs of the Rosetti children lining an upstairs hallway.

Of course, whether Ron would succeed at this game was beside the point. All that mattered to Jeanne were his intentions. With a contrived air of nonchalance, Jeanne sauntered through the dining-room area. She declined the round of invitations to blow on cards for good luck, sit on laps for better luck, or join the next hand to try her own luck with as much grace as she could manage, then whizzed through the opposite door leading into the kitchen.

The bright room was full of outdated olive-colored appliances and devoid of life, aside from Aunt Doreen. The stout, dark-haired woman had a blue gingham apron on over her holiday dress and was replenishing the food supply still spread out on the oval table. She met Jeanne on a return trip to the refrigerator. "Hungry, Jeanne?"

"Maybe a little," she fibbed, reaching for a soft, minty piece of taffy. She held it up before popping it into her mouth. "You pull this yourself?"

"No, there's a sweetshop in town. You should have Ron take you there tomorrow. Why, he and Elaine used to spend hours in there, back in the days when they had a soda fountain."

Jeanne nibbled at the candy. "I'm afraid we won't be around tomorrow."

"Aren't you staying the night? Everyone else is."

She paused. "Oh? First I heard of it."

Doreen clicked her tongue. "I wouldn't have been serving Ron all that rum if I'd known he intended to drive back."

"I'd better find out if we're staying. Have you seen Ron, Doreen?"

"He trotted through here with Elaine just a few minutes ago." She curled her fist. "Wait till I get my hands on that boy."

Jeanne curled a fist, too. Beautifully put.

Doreen filled a tray with drinks and cookies and headed for the dining room. Jeanne moved in the opposite direction, past the sink, toward the door into a hallway and the open staircase which led to the next level.

She started slowly down the dimly lit hallway. That was when she heard a squeal and a rumble coming from behind a closed door. A familiar, purry kind of rumble. It was a bedroom, too, the one where they'd stashed their things. Winding her arm up for the pitch, she lunged inside the room.

Unlike the hall, this room was well lit. And there stood Ron, holding Elaine in his arms. Kissing her for all he was worth.

10

"JEANNE!" the pair chorused, breaking apart.

Jeanne couldn't believe what happened next. Elaine was actually reaching for her—as if she could smooth things over! She quickly stepped back, speechless and furious. "Don't... let me bother you."

She wasn't sure where she got the poise, but Jeanne managed a sure-footed retreat, and slammed the door shut within inches of Ron's nose. The hinges creaked open immediately and she heard Ron's footsteps behind her.

"Jeanne!" he whispered. "Wait!"

"Keep quiet, you mean!" she whirled back to fling at him. She squinted in the dimness, frustrated that he didn't look terrified. Christmas music blared in the background, along with all the jolly human noises of those Jeanne suddenly perceived as blissfully naive. "I'm nothing but a cover, a front for your shenanigans!"

"That's silly."

Hissing a few well-chosen phrases she hadn't said or heard since her adolescence, she charged back into the kitchen and through a door she was certain led to the mudroom and the yard. Unfortunately, she found herself in a dark, stuffy, unfamiliar space.

Ron was chuckling as he joined her. "Jelly, anyone? Jam maybe? How about some pickles?"

"Huh?" She could feel his arm grazing her temple, and within seconds a bare bulb flicked on overhead. They were in a pantry about four feet square, surrounded by Doreen's canned goods. "Damn you, you beast!"

"Can I help it if you have no sense of direction?" He leaned against a shelf of peaches, a lazy smile on his lips. "Besides," he said more sternly, "this is no night to be running around outside. It must be close to zero by now."

Jeanne felt her eyes moisten and covered her face with her hands. "I think I hate you. I really think I do."

His eyes grew with the revelation. "Finally taking a stand, then?"

"What's that 'sposed to mean?"

He peeled her hands off her face with a growl. "I mean you've been avoiding all kinds of feeling for me. Until now. When you think the worst."

"Hah! And what about poor Tony and all the little Rosettis?" She extended her lower lip poutily.

"Don't change the subject. Let's talk about me and you."

She inhaled. "Okay. Let's talk about me, and how you decided I'm a replacement for Elaine—"

"Replacement?" he squawked in amazement.

"We do have a lot in common," she said bitingly. "Coloring, home-fire instincts."

"Oh, Jeanne." He exhaled and paused to choose the right words. "Look, I admit had I been ready way back when, Elaine would've been the one for me, but you're not a replacement. You're you. What I want now."

"But you just had to sample the old vintage, didn't you?"

"No," he denied hotly. "You're the one holding up the show here, walking on eggshells, reluctant to express yourself. I've tried so hard to get you to open up, and you lay this on me now of all times."

"Well, I don't hold my liquor very well," she explained defensively. "We Potters tend to express ourselves better while tipsy. But of course I've had feelings for you all along. Would I be here if I didn't?"

"You've made me feel like an intruder in your life from the start," he said angrily. "Made me feel like a reckless bum who breaks every heart in sight, and has a hungry eye on yours. Do you have any idea how much it upset me to hear you say that I finally needed you for a change? How could you miss the fact that I've needed and wanted you all along?"

She swallowed hard, as she absorbed the admission. "I guess I've been so wrapped up in my own situation, so frustrated by the trap set by my family, I haven't seen the clear picture."

"Helping you is what I needed to do," he sought to explain. "I needed to be needed, I guess you could say. It's been my pleasure to be there for you. I haven't had much experience in the giving department. I've been on my own so long with only myself to take care of."

"That's right," she fired back with a poke to his chest. "Your public image isn't a home-fires composite. Naturally I'd be cautious."

"But you should be over that by now!"

"How can you say that, when I just caught you with Elaine?"

"Forget Elaine till later. Trust me, it was nothing."

"Tony's the poor guy who will have to forget—"

"Hush!" He clamped a hand over her mouth, his brown eyes blazing. "Okay, here goes. When you returned the gift certificate to Gracie's, I went back to the store intending to return it. Lenora refused to give me a refund. I decided to shop for Emmett's gift there."

She wrenched his fingers off her mouth. "At Grace Brothers?"

"He's been behaving like a child, so it seemed fitting. Anyway, by providence I ran into Elaine there, for the first time in years. Jeanne, you should've seen her, with kids in tow, dressed in an ancient coat, disheveled as mothers sometimes are."

Jeanne blinked as her eyes moistened again. She had an idea of where he was headed.

"Anyhow, we talked, about Tony and his new garage. I realized money was tight—"

"And decided to give the certificate to her?"

"Indirectly. Lenora helped me."

Her features softened. "No wonder Lenora's so fond of you."

"Well, the rest is obvious. I paid Elaine for our part in this party and it reminded her that she wanted a showdown about that windfall in Gracie's. She dragged me into the bedroom—"

"Dragged? A first for you, I bet."

"Jeanne..." he muttered threateningly.

"Oops, old habit. Go on."

"She suspected the certificate deal was rigged from the start, and wanted to know if I was behind it. I confessed, and she was kissing me in thanks."

"Oh, Ron, I'm sorry."

"Tony knows all about it," he added dryly. "And to tell you the truth, I'm just as glad he decided not to kiss me, too. Now can we please forget about the Rosettis?"

"All right," she agreed quietly. "And if you're still interested, I do care for you."

"But why have you fought it so hard?"

"Because you weren't in the plan," she blurted out. "I had it in my head that I was going to get back in circulation after the holidays, and I thought I wanted a man like David." She shook her head dazedly. "I just didn't figure on falling in love at this time, especially with a man so different." She raised her palms in surrender. "But you've got me cornered every which way. Why, I was ready to duke it out with Elaine back there! Take it outside into the snow."

"Wow." He seized her in his arms then, and pulled her flush against him. "When you let go... wow!"

She sighed softly. "It's the Potter way. A little Christmas, a little rum and you've got yourself a basket case."

He pressed his lips to her hairline. "Oh, Jeanne, I absolutely adore you, honey. You drive me crazy, but I still can't resist the trip."

Her eyes grew large. "Is that the best smooch you can come up with?"

He rocked back on his heels. "'Fraid so. I kiss you anyplace else and I don't think we could walk out of here."

She instinctively smoothed her clothing. "That reminds me, Doreen wants to speak to you."

"Why?"

"Something about drinking and driving."

"Oh." He clearly understood.

"Seems everybody's accustomed to staying the night," she said scoldingly.

He nodded. "I didn't think you'd come at all if you knew about that tradition."

"I'm not sure we have a choice now. Both of us are unfit for the road."

"Can you manage, with Toby at Jason's?"

"Yes," she decided, glad that he thought to ask. "But I do think I'll give them a call and explain."

"Let's do it before it gets any later." Ever so gently, Ron eased open the pantry door a crack. He could see no one from his vantage point, so he hustled Jeanne out into the kitchen. Christmas tunes wafting in from the living room provided the background music for the expectant crowd hovering around the kitchen table, snacking with their fingers. Waiting for the closet show's dramatic climax.

Jeanne scanned them all with amazing aplomb. "There was no telephone in there, after all."

Chet, munching on a lemon bar, chuckled. "I swear, somebody ends up in that cupboard each and every year! Virtually soundproof, too, darn it."

Elaine sidled up to Jeanne with a captivating smile and shining green eyes. "You really need the phone?"

Jeanne smiled apologetically. "Yes. Not like me to take a wrong turn that way."

Elaine nodded, understanding and accepting her apology. "Calling the baby-sitter, I bet."

"Yes."

"Come along, there's a more private one in Uncle Chet's study."

The crowd dispersed thereafter. Some headed for the dining room parlor game, others drifted to the bedroom for their overnight totes.

"So, uh, do you have room for us to stay, Doreen?" Ron asked rather awkwardly.

"'Course we do," Doreen assured him with wink. "Up in that attic you helped me clean out fifteen years ago." Her voice dropped a notch. "Speak to Jeanne about the arrangements. If she prefers feminine company, I'll join her and you can bunk with Chet. A little cotton in your ears, and you won't notice the snoring half as much."

Ron rolled his eyes. Jeanne wouldn't do that to him, would she?

"GUESS WE'RE LUCKY to have a room to ourselves," Jeanne commented, sizing up the twin sleigh beds in the third story attic. Her eyes came to rest on the left one, on which Ron was stretched out beneath a pale yellow comforter, pillows propped against the sloping headboard. Presumably he'd stripped down to his skivvies. His white T-shirt was still pulled tight across his chest.

Ron smiled, thinking how lost she looked in Doreen's spare flannel nightie. "It's a full house all right. This space is the last choice because of the cold. I suppose it's tough to heat."

"You weren't even going to tell me about Doreen's offer, were you?" Jeanne said accusingly.

Ron stretched his strong arms with a groan. "Aw, gee, Jeanne. I couldn't stand to sleep with Chet. He snores and mumbles."

"Okay, okay." She shuffled closer. He flicked back his covers and moved to the far edge of the mattress.

"Come here, honey."

She stared at his body for a long, startled moment. Long, lean limbs, so strong and dark on the taut white sheet. "I don't know, Ron. If I'm ready, I mean..."

"We can at least hold each other, can't we? Keep warm?"

A soft sigh escaped her. David had been the only man she'd ever slept with. This kind of invitation was no doubt commonplace to Ron. And most single women her age probably wouldn't have a qualm. She finally cleared her throat. "You know my own nightie is a lot like this one."

As if he hadn't already guessed! She was a practical woman accustomed to dressing for her own convenience. Big deal. Couldn't she see that he liked her exactly as she was?

"You know what I'm driving at?" she asked tentatively.

He couldn't resist giving the matter the consideration she expected. "That you like being warm?"

"Well, yes, but—" She broke off, spotting the teasing glint in his eye.

He patted the mattress. "Me, too."

"But I wasn't expecting anything like this!"

"I wasn't either," he admitted gently. "Wasn't expecting to find myself caring so much for a woman that I'd be willing just to hold her through the night if that's all she wants." His handsome face grew dark with emotion. "I need you so close, so badly, Jeanne, that I'm willing to do it any way you say."

"Oh, Ron." With a surrendering moan she climbed in beside him. He swiftly closed the covers over them as though to seal her in.

He cradled her against his chest and buried his face in her hair. It smelled of the outdoors, woodsmoke and dinner. "I know this is all a spinning cyclone in your mind. That it's been tough to leave Toby overnight with the neighbor, venture into a group of my old friends. And now, end up in bed with me."

She quivered along his length, her softness sheer torture against his hard, sinewy muscles. He swallowed hard, struggling to keep his voice steady. "I would never pressure you..."

He wouldn't force her. But pressure? It was a natural part of his character. As she nuzzled her cheek into his rib cage, her mouth crooked in a smile.

"But if you'd be interested..." He trailed off in a tempting rumble.

She tipped her head up then, and planted her mouth on his for a featherlight taste. Ron wanted to take hold of her and pull her down for a grinding kiss. But he resisted. It had to be her move. Her choice.

The decision was a good one. Jeanne seemed to enjoy setting the pace. She set her hands on his chest and kissed him more deeply and wantonly. Lustily. There wasn't a nuance he missed.

The way her breasts were crushing against his ribs.

The way her hands were grasping his hips.

The way her thigh was nudging his groin.

The way she was climbing on top of him...

With a groan he stretched out flat on the bed. Her mating moves were so slow and so subtle, he felt he had to be dreaming. And the forever kind of kiss went on and on throughout. Their slicked lips slid over each other's, whetting their appetites.

Ron's control was slipping. Confident that she was willing and ready, he ever-so-gently pulled her nightgown up over her head and tossed it aside. With a desire-roughened touch, he skimmed his hands over her silky back, massaged her hips, clenched her bottom. His erection was rigid behind the cotton barrier of his briefs. Over and over again, he pushed her groin into his with a pressure-packed undulation.

Jeanne inched up his T-shirt, tugged it off, and began nibbling at his nipples, She licked and nipped them to sensitive pebbles in the chilly room, and caressed his skin with bolder and bolder strokes. With a shiver, Ron pulled the covers over their shoulders. As he did so he could feel her fingers on the elastic of his briefs, inching them down. She caught them with her toes at midthigh, then pulled them clean off with sort of a flutter kick. Their naked bodies rubbing together made them shiver with anticipation.

Tipping his head up, Ron lost himself in the softness of her breasts. Her heart pounding wildly in her chest made him think of a new and unsure filly. But all she needed was encouragement, assurances that she was all he wanted in this world. A flame to reignite her fuse.

With an abruptness that jolted him to the core of his being, she suddenly arched and swallowed his shaft in her feminine opening.

The moist grazing friction made them both gasp and quake.

"You witch," he uttered hoarsely, blinking up into her eyes of blue fire.

The fuse was lit all right.

Clamping his hands to her hipbones, he raised and lowered her over him.

Jeanne grasped his arms for balance, entranced by his strength, the tantalizing, burning rub of their bodies. And the motions. Faster and faster their bodies moved together until their passions reached a pinnacle.

Jeanne's slender spine arched back, her hair tumbled in a golden shimmer and she cried out ever so softly in complete fulfillment. Ron climaxed soon after with a guttural, masculine, triumphant sound.

She collapsed on his heaving chest to share a deep carnal kiss as their breathing slowed. Finally she rested her head in the curve of his shoulder.

He reached up and rapped his knuckle on the curving headboard. "Now, didn't I promise you a fun ride? And you, lucky lady, ended up with two!"

Jeanne laughed, bending the pillow into his face. "Get too smart and you'll end up in the barn—in the other sleigh."

He chuckled deep and low, and drew her under the quilt. "Just try and get rid of me now. Give me some more of that body rub. I dare ya."

So she did.

11

"GOOD MORNING, POP." Ron glanced up from his laptop computer as Emmett appeared in the kitchen doorway, still dressed in his silk pajamas. "Getting off to a slow start, eh?"

Emmett yawned hugely. "Well, it is a Saturday. What time is it?"

"Nearly ten." Ron motioned with his disheveled brown head toward the side counter. "There's some fresh coffee there."

Emmett helped himself to a mug. "Aren't *we* chipper," he observed in dry surprise. "And ambitious. Out all night and straight on to work."

"Got a fair amount of sleep. Enough to last me." Ron paused pensively, wondering if in truth he could ever get enough sack time with Jeanne. The ritual of intense, impetuous sex followed by a deep, sound sleep was one he could easily grow accustomed to. "Anyway, I have to stick with this article for Burt Waters over at the *Clarion*. Tomorrow's my deadline."

"So you decided on a title?"

"Recapturing the Spirit of Home." Ron noted Emmett's approving noises, then went back to typing. "Yesterday's reunion gave me the insight I needed to finish. So glad I went."

"Did you stay up at the orchard with Elaine's relatives?"

"Everybody did, just like the old days."

"Jeanne have a good time?"

Ron struggled to keep his expression indifferent. "Oh, I think so."

Emmett rummaged through his bread box, and pulled out a loaf of whole-wheat. "Yes, I scored myself last night."

Ron's fingers flew up from the keys. "Better watch your terms, Pop. Might land you in trouble."

Emmett regarded him crossly. "Your ears suddenly delicate? Frostbitten, maybe?"

"I mean you wouldn't want to slip in front of Jeanne or Lenora. They're irreplaceable."

"Yes, right. But we lads are alone, aren't we?"

"Yes, it does seem to be our condition too often." Ron made a show of returning to the keyboard. Hopefully, Emmett would drop the issue.

Emmett moved closer, though, his pale eyes bright with curiosity. "So you going to marry this Jeanne?"

Ron met his gaze smugly. "You marryin' Lenora?"

Emmett arched like a mighty eagle. Ron prepared himself for a lengthy lecture.

"Asked you first," the old man said childishly.

Ron roared with laughter. "I expect an applause-getting soliloquy and get, 'asked you first?'"

"Well, I did. And I expect an answer."

"To be honest, I just don't know yet." Ron steepled his fingers and used them to prop his chin. "But it's very possible."

Pleased with himself and the news, Emmett wandered over to the counter and set two pieces of bread in the toaster. "Well, I have to admit you were right about Lenora's being quite a dish. But in my case, I'm not so sure about a legal knot. It's so important, picking a mate for life!"

Ron made a thoughtful sound. "Tough decision. She is about twenty years younger than you are. Probably has a bit more zip, and a more active life-style. And she's liable to work full-time for another few years, until she's sixty-five."

"Are you insinuating that she might not be ready and willing to accept my proposal, if I choose to make one? Why—" Emmett paused in midstorm. "Oh, yes, see what you mean. She might not see me as the catch of the year."

"Then again, she might," Ron returned kindly. "I just think you should give her the option."

"Agh, sometimes I forget I'm eighty."

"So do I," Ron agreed. "One day you seem five, the next fifty, then seventy. You're all over the map."

"Still, you're right. A little humility with a hot babe like Lenora might help the cause." He brought his toast to the table and sat beside his grandson. "Speaking of things hot, son, I'd like that photo Jeanne took of Lenora on my knee."

Ron chuckled in reminiscence. "Jeanne is having some copies made for you."

Emmett brightened. "Good. Saves me the trouble."

"Oh, by the way, thanks for picking up Toby's toys."

Emmett sniffed. "Nothing to it. That reminds me, though. The mother called."

Ron's jaw tightened. "Catherine?"

"Yes. She certainly is bubbly, isn't she?"

"But she's trouble for us right now, Pop. If she comes to realize that you're the no-good Santa who spoke to Toby, we'll both be done for."

"Find her quite irresistible just the same," Emmett went on grandly.

"So, what did she want?"

"Wanted to know if she could come over and wrap Toby's presents. Gave me a delightful line of patter about how all the gifts should be done up in the same paper, with a neatness worthy of Mrs. Claus. If you ask me, I think she's angling to get to know us better."

"Hope you said no."

"Naturally. And most regrettably. I covered by saying that she might as well hold off until you've unearthed the last items."

"Perfect answer, Pop."

"So, how many more scribbles are left?"

"Well, presuming that I'm right about the hoop, two."

"Better hurry up."

"I'm trying to, Pop. Christmas Eve is next Tuesday, and Jeanne definitely needs all the stuff by then."

"No, I mean you'd better hurry the romance. Once you deliver up the goods, you may be kicked out of the nest."

Ron glared at him. "I might be tempted to make a romantic call if you felt the compulsion to shave or something."

Emmett laboriously got to his feet and shuffled off agreeably. What he didn't know was that Ron had been putting off this call for a couple of hours. If Jeanne was regretting their fantasy evening he was in no hurry to find out.

"Closing the bathroom door now!" Emmett called out.

"That's the last progress report I want to hear out that bathroom, Romeo!" Taking a bolstering breath, he picked up the receiver pressed Jeanne's number and waited anxiously as her phone rang.

"MOMM-E-E-E, Ronny wants to talk to you."

Jeanne sat up straight in the bathtub. "Is he at the door?"

"On the phone, Mommy." The doorknob jiggled. "You locked you in."

She smiled wryly. "Oh, sorry, champ."

There was a faint thumping sound near the floor. "Phone won't fit under, Mommy."

"Toby, where is Angie?"

"Right here" came her sister's muffled response.

"Hang on, I'm coming out."

Jeanne whisked open the door seconds later, wrapped in a bulky pink fleece robe. She stared anxiously at Angie's empty hands. "Where is the telephone?"

The normally confident big sister was looking altogether frazzled and embarrassed. "Toby ran away with it."

"Oh, Angie!"

"He doesn't listen to anything I say," Angie complained loudly.

With a huff of disgust, Jeanne flounced down the hallway. "How can you let that child outfox you all the time?"

Angie trailed after her sister. "I can't help it. I tried to make cleaning out your refrigerator a game."

Jeanne stopped in the foyer, and spun around in amazement. "Cleaning out my what?"

"It was a real disaster," Angie claimed. "Tossing in a box of baking soda every six months isn't a cure-all."

Jeanne raised a finger to defend her fridge, but decided against a tongue-lashing. She'd save her energy to deal with Ron's smooth tongue. The things it said, the places it went. Her damp body shivered beneath her robe.

Angie noticed her condition, and promptly misjudged the cause. "You're going to catch a cold, half wet, half dressed."

"Oh, go—" Jeanne sputtered in frustration. "Go clean out the freezer section!"

Angie saluted with glee. "Yes, ma'am!" With a click of her heels she was off to the kitchen.

Toby was clearly visible from the foyer. He was standing in the living room near the Christmas tree in his Disney-print pajamas, clutching the cordless phone, his blond head bobbing as he told Ron all about Jason's tree and how the Trent's was so much better. Jeanne listened from the doorway for a few minutes, convinced that Toby was in heaven.

It seemed only fair, since she'd been there for hours last night.

Finally, when Toby seemed to be repeating himself, she stepped up to take the instrument from him. "Hi, Ron."

"Hi, yourself."

"Did I catch you at a bad time?"

"No—yes. I mean, well, I have a grueling day ahead." She closed her eyes, knowing how clipped she sounded. But it was the circumstances, not the company. "After playing yesterday, I really have to keep the old nose to the grindstone today."

"Oh."

She paced round the room, biting her lip. "I'm sorry. I just get like this under pressure."

"Been there, done that," he said with forced cheer.

"So, you understand?" she asked hopefully.

"Of course. Any chance of a break later? I'd like to come over, spend some time with Toby, finish off that scavenger hunt."

"Not today, Ron. I just won't have a single minute today."

"Tonight, then."

"Even worse!" she lamented, rubbing her forehead.

"I suppose I could finish up my article for the newspaper," he said grumpily.

"Sounds like a good idea," she enthused. "Keep you busy."

"About last night, Jeanne. Doesn't it seem like—"

"A million miles away?" she finished, as she reached for a stray sock wedged between two sofa cushions.

"I was going to call it magic."

She squeezed the receiver, her voice dropping to a whisper. "It was really special for me, too. But you know how—"

"Know what!"

She winced at the thunder in his voice. "That I have so much on my mind in the upcoming days. Obligations."

"Well, if you're really busy—"

"I am. Look, I have to go. Toby's carrying a five-quart bucket of ice cream around the house. Toby, it's breakfast time!" she shouted. Then on a note of regret she closed with a simple, "'Bye, Ron."

"Ice cream?" Ron slammed down the telephone with force. "Why the kid couldn't begin to reach the freezer door handle. What a dumb excuse. What a dumb lie!"

Emmett, now freshly shaven and in his street clothes, peered into the kitchen. "Everybody going out for ice cream?"

"No, Pop. Nobody's going anywhere."

RON KEPT TELLING himself he was going no place. Lenora stopped by on her lunch hour to pick Emmett up for work, which gave Ron some badly needed peace and quiet. And in a rush of inspiration he finished his article for the *Clarion*.

Suddenly he had all the time in the world to think about Jeanne, to mull over their quick and unexpected courtship.

With nothing better to do, he decided to transcribe his handwritten journal to a computer disk. Edit it, condense it, and at the same time review, decide if this was where he wanted to be headed. It would be like taking a journey without ever leaving the high-rise.

He spent the afternoon typing, sorting, thinking. And it made him all the more certain of his feelings for Jeanne. But the exercise had its downside. As dusk set in, he wasn't sure he could get through the night without seeing her. Passion and irritation welled inside him as he packed up his computer and papers. He stuffed the works haphazardly on the top of Emmett's bookshelf.

If only she were free.

She couldn't help it if she was working.

He'd only be in the way.

If she was really working and not simply hiding from him.

She had enjoyed the intimacy.

But had she been as ready as she seemed?

She'd never lie to him, never just dump him.

By six o'clock he was behind the wheel of the Plymouth. If she'd lost the magic, he'd just have to help her find it again.

THE LAST THING Ron expected was a traffic jam on Jeanne's small, suburban street. Cars flanked the curbs, wedged into the tightest spots imaginable.

It appeared that somebody was having one hell of a Christmas bash.

Ron crawled along the street at a snail's pace, planning how he'd pull up in her driveway and park off to the side in case she had a customer or two who needed a spot.

His plan was short-lived. The Trent driveway was already crammed with cars, and was the only one on the street in that condition. Apparently Jeanne was the one having the Christmas bash!

Ron's foot hovered over the accelerator. He was tempted to zoom off, nurse his wounds at an old familiar bar someplace—where the women would be happy to see him, and no doubt cooperative.

But he just couldn't do it. He couldn't let this go. He'd introduced her to his friends, and listened sympathetically to the story that she didn't see many of her old friends because of her widowhood.

Well, somebody was hanging around. Every light blazed in the house and music rocked the foundations. It seemed everyone was there but the cops—and him. He hung a left at the corner and slipped into the first available space.

He stalked down the sidewalk, barrelled around the corner and almost collided with a little man walking his dog. He apologized and kept on moving.

Was a pattern forming? he wondered as he jabbed the doorbell. Again, he was standing on this stoop, hopping mad. This time she wouldn't smooth things over with a limpid look. Nosirree.

Nobody answered the bell. As he was jabbing it for the fifth time the inside door opened. A young man of eighteen or twenty stared suspiciously at Ron. Then the storm door creaked open a crack.

"Where's Jeanne?"

"You sellin' something, buddy?"

Ron bared his white teeth. "No, buddy."

"You the brother?"

"No!"

Ron gritted his teeth in disappointment. Obviously this wasn't Jeanne's little brother Andrew. So, who was the young whip who seemed so overly protective of Jeanne? The kid edged his head and shoulders into view and Ron's eyes widened. He was wearing a tuxedo!

Young, but old enough, Ron surmised.

"She expecting you, or what?"

"Or what." Ron pushed past the kid, charged into the foyer and came to a quick halt. The place was crawling with couples in formal wear. He was out of place in his forest-green sweater, black jeans and blue ski jacket. What was going on here? He felt ancient. The kid who answered the door was on the threshold of manhood, but the majority of these other males were still battling acne!

He didn't notice Jeanne until she was right beside him.

"Good evening."

"Uh, good evening." Ron's eyes roved over her figure. She was dressed more casually than he was, in a mint sweatshirt and faded denims. But she looked every bit as harassed.

"You're upsetting the flow," she told him with a toss of her head.

Ron's brows jumped a mile. "Huh?"

"Oh, come on."

As she tugged him along by the elbow, Ron was vaguely aware of the teenage girls in candy-colored gowns staring at him. In a hungry, dreamy-eyed way that added to his embarrassment.

"This is Ron," Jeanne called out above the racket.

A very pretty Oriental girl dressed in rose taffeta inspected him from the studio doorway. "Is he yours, Jeanne?"

Jeanne blushed. "Well, yes, Jaclyn, I guess so. Wild-eyed and shaggy-haired and all."

"I would've come in black tie had I known," Ron announced evenly.

Jaclyn's slanted dark eyes danced merrily. "Never mind. You're way cool as you are!" She swished off to spread the news. Widow Jeanne was back in circulation. And had landed a hunk.

"Just look what you've done!" Jeanne chided, throwing her hands up in the air as she flew into her studio.

Ron followed. Amazingly, this room was empty. But it was obvious that a photo shoot was planned. An ice-castle backdrop covered the back wall, and a camera was set up on the tripod, ready for action. Jeanne closed the door behind them with a firm shove.

"What did I do?" he repeated. "I think what I did was polish up your image."

To his surprise she laughed. "Yes, along with disrupting my well-tuned schedule. The least you can do is explain why you've come in the first place."

"Would you believe I happened to be in the neighborhood?"

Her small mouth twitched. "Maybe..."

"And couldn't resist stopping by?"

She squinted at him. "You looked ready to beat somebody up."

He balled his fists. "Okay, okay, I was ticked and anxious about your brush-off and decided to come over. And subsequently went nuts when I figured you were having a party without me. Satisfied?"

With a throaty chuckle she cuddled up close, and eased her arms around his middle underneath his ski jacket. "Happy, grateful, but not at all satisfied." She stood on tiptoe to give him a long, luxurious kiss. "Oh, Ron, this is the nicest gift you could've given me right now. Caring enough to be jealous."

Ron's hands skimmed her hourglass waistline and the base of her spine, and gently pushed her belly into his. "We've been all through this, honey. I'm hooked."

"I know. Still..."

"I do understand," he crooned in her ear. "Last night we were tipsy and needy." He hugged her fiercely. "But it's all the more real to me today. And I simply needed to hear the same from you. In person."

"That's exactly right, darling." She rested her head on his chest, the rhythm of his hammering heart the sweetest music imaginable. "Exactly how I feel, too."

"So why didn't you want me around today?"

She raised her head to look at him. "Because you're just too distracting!"

"What is going on here?" he asked hoarsely. "And how can we make them go away?"

"We can't," she said with a heartfelt sigh. "This happens to be my biggest money-maker of the year. "Pictures for Rigby High's Snowflake Dance."

"Like prom pictures?"

"Yes. Another gold-mine event for area photographers. I'm hoping, with time, I'll garner some contracts for proms from area schools. But right now, all I have is Rigby's Snowflake. It's my third year at it."

Ron looked around again. "You herd the couples in here one by one and shoot them? Must take forever."

She glanced at the clock on the wall. "Yes, and it's time I got started."

The door opened suddenly and Toby raced in, a cherub-faced terror in tennis shoes, dungaree coveralls and a festive candy-stripe T-shirt. "Where's my hat? I need the hat to be the helper." His eyes grew round as he spotted Ron. "Hey, Ronny! You come!"

"Sure, sport."

The boy scampered over to wedge himself between the adults. Ron picked him up and gave a twirl in the air. Toby squealed in delight.

Jeanne reached for her spare camera on the desk and took some quick shots of the pair, then struggled to look stern. "Now, boys, it's time for work."

Toby's hazel eyes were huge as Ron set him down. "My hat!"

"Is this it?" Ron moved to the desk where he'd spotted a red-velvet Santa's hat trimmed with fur. Toby nodded, so Ron bent over and placed it on the child's crown of fluffy blond hair. The tip of the hat had a bell that tinkled every time Toby bobbed his head.

Jeanne clapped her hands. "You, Toby, go tell the kids to line up. You, Ronny, go into the kitchen for Angie."

"She's here to help? I'm not, but she is?"

Jeanne gestured toward the bathroom. "Do you know anything about hair and makeup?"

Ron gazed into the brightly lit room and realized that it was set up like a beauty salon. "Not a thing."

"Then move out. Sit in the kitchen and have a glass of wine."

Ron obeyed. Halfway down the hall he collided with Angie, a purple streak in sweats. "You're needed," he informed her merrily. "Like right now."

"You're needed yourself, Ron Coleman," she returned candidly. "Like today and tomorrow and forever."

He gave her arm a pat. "Just try and get rid of me."

"I just want you to understand how fragile Jeanne is."

"I know," he said solemnly.

"Angie, get your hiney in here!" Jeanne appeared in the studio doorway, fists clenched, screeching at the top of her lungs.

"Fragile as crystal underneath," Angie mouthed hurriedly before dashing off.

Ron was still smiling as he sauntered into the kitchen, pleasantly lost in his thoughts. The idea of finding peace over a solitary glass of some fine vintage was a foolishly shortsighted one. He was confronted with a tidal wave of season's greetings. From all the Potters! Catherine and Martin, and a man promptly introduced as Angie's husband, Brad, were seated around the table with a huge bottle of cheap wine and platters of snacks.

No wonder the schoolboy had mistaken him for brother Andrew. He was the only missing link!

"Oh, Ron, you felt you should be here in support, too." Catherine gushed, steering him to an empty chair.

Here in support? He could see why Jeanne was so nervous. Not only did she have a job to do, she had all her overprotective guardian angels hovering by. "Busy place tonight," he said simply, reaching for a large brownie.

"You must be hungry," Martin observed. "Get him a plate, Cat."

"Of course." Catherine bustled to the cupboard. "Did you have dinner, Ron? Bet you didn't. I can tell. Try some of the veggie dip. And those ham slices are fresh from the deli."

"Wonder if Jeanne is ready for a plate," Brad mused. "Something without a lot of sugar to harm her teeth."

"No, I don't think so," Ron said quickly as he loaded his own plate.

Martin poured him a glass of wine, which Ron gratefully accepted.

"Been busy today?" Catherine asked solicitously. "You and your charming grandfather?"

If only he could continue to steer her away from Emmett. He took a large gulp of wine. "I've been writing all day," he told them. "That article for the Minneapolis *Clarion*."

"But we live in St. Paul!" Martin thundered. "So does Emmett."

Ron chuckled, familiar with the rivalry between the cities. "I grew up in Minneapolis, though. Know a guy on the paper."

"Tell us about the article," Catherine urged, leaning over the table.

He did so between bites. He explained that it was about returning to one's hometown, and seeing its qualities through wiser eyes. "It's scheduled for the Monday edition."

"We will buy a dozen copies," Martin bellowed in delight. "Maybe two dozen."

Ron, soaking up their interest and admission, decided he just might enjoy being a Potter by proxy more than he'd thought.

Jeanne appeared in the kitchen ninety minutes later, looking weary but relieved. "I can use some help now, with the picking up."

A round of groans filled the air.

"Like always, there are some dirt stains on the carpet and smudges on the walls. And, heaven only knows, why all my decorative pillows are stuffed in the oddest places!"

Angie appeared behind her baby sister, clapping her hands. "C'mon, people, you can't expect me to do it all."

Grumbles that she was more than capable followed. But everyone rose and marched to the battle areas.

Ron and Jeanne lingered behind.

"Sorry you came?" she asked.

"Not at all." With a deep groan, he gathered her close. "I like your family."

"And they adore you." She stood on tiptoe to lick some sugar from the side of his mouth. The act soon turned into a deep, heady kiss, a swift stolen moment that both knew would have to last them the night.

Toby bounced into view, his hat ajingle. "Hey, everybody, they're stealin' smooches again!"

"Hey, everybody," Ron growled against her mouth. "I'm collecting my candy-cane kisses."

12

"SEEMS IT WAS your turn to sleep in," Emmett observed dryly as Ron stumbled into the kitchen bleary-eyed, dressed only in his underwear.

"It *is* Sunday," Ron said, mimicking the excuse Emmett had used the day before.

Emmett poured him coffee, then settled down in his favorite easy chair before the television set. Ron smirked when he realized *It's A Wonderful Life* was on the air. Emmett had always coveted the Jimmy Stewart role and attempted to critique the actor's fine performance year after year. The Potters weren't the only ones with Christmas spirit and tradition!

"Have a nice evening, Ron?"

"Yes, even got another gift item out of Toby. A bulldozer for his sandbox."

Emmett toasted him with his mug. "Well done."

"Wasn't due to my skills, really," Ron admitted, sinking into the *Hamlet* chair. "I was tucking him into bed, and he was rambling on about his new best friend Jason, and it just popped out that they'd both be moving piles of dirt around this spring. Thought I'd pick it up at Grace Brothers this afternoon when I drop you off."

Emmett nodded. "Did you speak to Jeanne about the photo?"

"Yes, and she said the copies would be ready today."

"Splendid, splendid!"

"You're welcome, Pop," Ron teased.

Emmett lifted his shoulders in a way that made his emerald robe shimmer. "As usual, we do favors for each other."

Ron arched a brow. "Meaning?"

"Meaning that Burt from the newspaper sent a messenger for your story."

"You should've gotten me up!"

"I didn't have the heart. You looked so peaceful. Anyway, the disk was right there on the shelf."

Ron jumped up, sloshing coffee on his bare thigh, and raced to the bookshelf. Sure enough, the disk he'd set atop his stuff was missing. "You gave him the red disk, not the yellow one."

"Yes, the one marked, *Clarion*."

"Good work. The other one's my journal. I was condensing it for fun."

Emmett rolled his eyes. "Sounds like a real gas."

"It was very satisfying," Ron insisted. "I've never been so in love and I enjoyed thinking and writing about all the things that have happened, and the way they all happened."

Emmett snorted and returned to his movie, and Ron went for a second cup of coffee. Both were startled by a sharp rap on the high-rise's entry door.

"Now who could that be?" Emmett rose slowly and ambled over to the peephole.

Ron, in no condition to greet callers in his skivvies, peered out of the kitchen, ready to dash to the bedroom. "So who is it?"

"Why, it's her!" Emmett rejoiced, admiration in his tone.

Ron scowled and hissed. "Her who?"

"The cheeky one. Cat."

Ron was a streak of tanned skin as he escaped to his room.

He reappeared minutes later dressed in the first thing he could put his hands on, his gray workout sweats. Catherine had taken far greater care with her appearance. Her flaxen hair was done up in a neat little knot, there was a dash of color on her high cheekbones, and her turquoise blouse and dark trousers were pressed to perfection. She was still a fine-looking woman. It was like looking at Jeanne twenty-five years from now.

His Christmas future. It warmed Ron to think of it. He wouldn't be a crusty old bachelor, after all. He'd be a doddering old husband, still foolishly in love.

"There you are, sleepyhead!" Catherine nodded at him from the dinnette area, a pair of scissors in her hand and rolls of snowman-figured paper piled on the table. It was clear she'd come to wrap Toby's presents.

"Morning, Cat."

Catherine looked around at her helper. "Get my tote, Emmer, over on the chair. There's ribbon, and tape, and lord only knows what else inside!"

Ron sidled over to nudge Emmett with his elbow. *Emmer?* he mouthed out of Catherine's vision.

The old man brushed him off like a pesky fly. "We're busy as blazes here. Help or get lost."

Ron gathered up Toby's gifts in the guest room, and hauled them to the dinette. Catherine eyed the remote-control car box, then unrolled some wrap. "Oh, yes, Emmer, there's a brown envelope in the tote for you from Jeanne."

Ron and Emmett exchanged a horrified look, and raced each other to the bag. Jeanne had sent along the photos of Emmett as Santa? Emmett's withered hand dipped into the tote and produced the eight-by-ten envelope. The men's expressions grew relieved. It was closed and crisscrossed with masking tape, impervious to snoops.

Catherine watched them curiously. "Seems rather large for a Christmas card. It's about the size of an eight-by-ten glossy."

"Maybe it's one of the photos she took of me with Toby," Ron improvised. "A holiday thing."

"We had a photo taken of Toby with Santa, you know," Catherine confided huffily. "But after all the fuss, Jeanne simply put it aside, won't even let me see it again."

"Jeanne knows best, I'm sure," Ron said. "Did I tell you I'm going to get that bulldozer this afternoon?"

"Yes, you told me last night." Catherine snapped her fingers, and pointed to the envelope. "Well, let's have a look."

"When we have all this work to do?" Emmett squared his shoulders and the deep voice that thrilled audiences filled the room.

Catherine's pretty blue eyes clouded. "You know, there's something about the way you lift your chin, and your voice when you speak out like that." She shook her head. "I'm sure I know you."

The men mumbled and turned away. Catherine shrugged and got back to work.

"So what is Jeanne up to today?" Ron asked. He'd moved to the table to hold corners as Catherine efficiently taped them.

"Oh, she and Toby are over at our place. Andrew's home from college—arrived at about six this morning. We had every minute of these days planned before you appeared, Ron. We wanted to keep Jeanne as cheery and busy as possible." She sighed, pressing a hand to her chest. "Jeanne is such a loyal kind of person. The type to make a commitment and stick to it. We had recommended that she play the field a bit before falling so hard for one man again. But here are the two of you, all locked up, heart and soul. I mean, you do love her back, don't you?"

"Yes, Catherine, I most sincerely do."

"Yes. Well, then it's all right then, isn't it?"

"It's all right," he assured her with twinkling eyes. "It's never been more all right."

"Oh, oh, what a merry Christmas for all of us!" Emmett bellowed, bouncing Ron the basketball.

Catherine's back arched and her scissors stopped on the paper in midsnip. Ever so slowly she stood up to her full height, and turned to Emmett. "Repeat what you said," she requested crisply.

"Whatever do you mean, Cat?" Emmett asked guilelessly, still the first-class stage performer.

"Change those oh-ohs to ho-hos, if you please."

"Rather not strain my voice, dear lady."

"Go ahead, anyway. Make my day." Squinting meanly she raised the hand holding the shears and advanced toward the old man. Ron gently caught her wrist and disarmed her. "I'll wrap the basketball."

She forged on, her fingers now pointing accusingly. "You!"

"Me?" Emmett's tone was a silken bedroom baritone.

"I thought Jeanne was trying to keep us apart, and now I'm beginning to understand why. And I'll just bet that whatever's in that envelope proves my point."

"Point?" Ron croaked. The ball slipped from his fingers, and bounced to the kitchen, making a plopping sound in the electrified silence.

"Jeanne was behaving very strangely about that envelope. Didn't want me to see inside it." Before either male could stop her, she had snatched it from the coffee table, and was tearing away the layers of tape. Glossy eight-by-tens spilled out on the carpet. Images of Ron and Toby with the red-velvet hat were unfortunately followed by snaps of Emmett in all his jolly glory, holding tight to a startled Lenora. Catherine wasted no time snatching up a copy of the latter. "Ah-ha! It's true!"

"Now, Catherine," Ron began slowly, putting out his hands.

An agonized sound erupted from the depths of her throat. "Do you know what you've done to us, making Toby those promises?"

Ron stepped in front of his grandfather, whose facade was crumbling. "We've already settled this with Jeanne."

"Have you really!" It was more an exclamation of disgust than a query. "Jeanne said she was taking care of it—but—but this is how?" Catherine shook a fist at Emmett.

"You know I'm doing my level best to get the answers out of the child," Ron said reasonably.

"But it's the old man here who has the power to fix things to make a retraction!"

"Santa does not renege," Emmett said loftily from behind Ron's solid shoulder.

Ron stifled a laugh. "Catherine, everything is under control, honestly."

"Is it? What's the last scribble mean? You have all the others, but not the last one. The one that Toby's least likely to talk about."

Ron sobered. "I'll find out. I promise!"

"No, you won't," she spat furiously. Grabbing her tote, she shoveled all her supplies inside. "I'm taking these gifts along as planned. And don't you dare try and stop me. Don't you dare!"

The men carried the stuff into the hallway for her. She went off on the first of the two necessary trips to her car.

"Maybe you should try and stop her," Emmett suggested, sagging against the corridor wall. "From leaving altogether."

"Stop a Potter?" Ron raked his hands through his shaggy hair. "If I tried she'd probably gleefully add forcible confinement to our crimes."

"Very well." With a regal sniff he disappeared into the apartment.

Ron paced the floor for the next two hours. He called Jeanne's house several times, but there was no answer. Of course she was at the family compound, whooping it up with her brother and the rest. At least they would have been whooping it up until Catherine burst in on the scene. She'd probably be furious with Jeanne because Jeanne had kept Emmett's identity secret to protect Ron. The Potters wouldn't appreciate that kind of insubordination.

If only Ron could fix the situation. What would be the wisest next move? He paused at the window, overlooking Como Avenue, watching the snow fall ever so gently to the ancient trees below. For a moment he relived the chilly glory of their sleigh ride, the laughter, the carols, the second sleigh ride. They'd created their own Christmas card that night. Romantic perfection.

But all in all he should have known better than to expect an idyllic repeat of Christmas Past, of days as carefree as those of childhood. Christmas might very well be just for youngsters, after all.

The telephone rang during his musings. He picked up on the second ring.

"Oh, Ron! Thank goodness you're there!"

"Jeanne. Thank goodness you called." His voice cracked with relief. "I tried your house. Believe me, I'm so sorry for what happened."

"I'm sure you are," she crooned in sympathy.

"And rest assured, I'm here for you."

There was a pause on the line. "What I want to say, Ron, is that you're best off right where you are."

"Huh?"

"I mean, I'm glad you had the sense not to go to my folks', or come to my house."

His lean features darkened. "Jeanne, you can't mean it."

"The family's in an uproar. Everything's a mess."

"Is Catherine angry with you for shielding Emmett?" he asked tightly.

"Yes, a little. But they're busier plotting damage control, fuming over you and Emmett," she finished in a small voice.

"Oh." The single word response sounded flat and discouraged.

"You can't be surprised, Ron," she said almost accusingly.

"If only you'd stopped her from coming here, Jeanne."

"I tried. But she's impossible. You know firsthand how impossible."

"I can't help but be a little angry myself," he said hotly. "I've run myself ragged trying to set this right for Toby, and court you, and it all blows up in my face right before Christmas."

"I think you're being selfish here," she snapped.

"No, I'm not," he countered, his voice rising. "A little more time and I'd have been the hero. I'd have found the last thing on Toby's list. All I needed was another day."

"You don't know that, Ron! Nobody but Toby knows what that last wish is. Nobody knows if you could've made it come true."

He hooted in disbelief. "But just yesterday you were satisfied with my efforts. Thought I could do anything and everything!"

Her voice caught in a small sob. "I'm so sorry, Ron. This is a lot my own fault, for sure. Maybe I was wrong to let myself fall in love again so soon."

"That isn't wrong!"

"It hasn't worked out at all, though. My family's a wreck. They're trying to question Toby and he doesn't understand. He thinks they're crazy."

"He understands very well then, in my opinion!"

"How dare you! With a loony grandfather who believes he's Santa Claus!"

"Oh, Jeanne. Let's not—"

"You know what I'm leading up to," she cut in sharply. "We simply have to end things here. Before we get in too deep."

"Before—" He was already drowning in his passions, his dreams. "But we love each other!" he roared.

"We hardly know each other."

"Not so," he insisted.

"A little corner of my mind still is unsure," she admitted. "About a future with a man so different."

"Different from David?"

"Well, yes!"

Ron felt his very soul was on fire. How could he compete with a memory? "How would he have handled all of this?"

"He would've throttled his grandfather into submission for starters," she readily replied.

"I just couldn't, Jeanne. It isn't our way."

"I know. David's from no-nonsense stock. And you, Ron, you're from—from summer stock!"

"Has it occurred to you that we come from the same kind of stubborn, high-spirited people?"

"Of course it has! And it spells dynamite dynamics. All the more reason to make sure the feelings are lasting, before we incinerate each other."

"I can't replace the even-keeled David, Jeanne," he replied tersely. "I won't try to whip Emmett into shape, either. All I can do is offer to settle down with a woman I adore and light her fire in my own unique way. If, all things considered, you're looking for a David Trent replacement, you're out of luck. It's your decision."

She made it, too. She hung up.

Realizing it was time for Emmett to get to the store, Ron quickly changed into a shirt and slacks, then tracked the old man down in his bedroom. To his amazement, Emmett was back in bed, the covers crowded up around his throat as though he had a chill.

"I just can't go in today, son," he said feebly.

Ron clenched his fists. "The last thing I need is another crisis!"

"I know, I heard your side of the battle." Emmett's head lolled on the pillows. "I'm dreadfully sorry, but I've decided my portrayal of jolly old St. Nick is completely unappreciated. The Potters hate me and Stanley Bickel would prefer to replace me with an unprofessional hack. All in all, I have lost the will to do the part justice."

Ron circled the bed like an anxious physician. "You said yourself that Jeanne's complaint was the only one. That should give you the confidence to fulfill your contract."

"No, the spark is gone. Go to the store and explain, will you?"

"I'll call Stanley," Ron suggested.

"No, son. Go in and speak to him in person." He pursed his dry and trembling lips. "Don't want him to sue."

"Oh, all right." Ron turned to leave, but Emmett grasped his hand. "The family circus is clouding the issue. I feel that Jeanne's biggest problem is her fear that you're not the marrying kind. That you'd grow tired of her and Toby. If only you'd concentrate on that angle. Try to convince her."

Ron's gaze was hooded, his voice curt. "I gave it my best. She has no excuse for doubts. She's seen me at my most sincere and that is that." With that parting shot, he fled the room.

"Yeah, yeah, just as I figured," Emmett grumbled to himself. "A chip off the old block. In communications, but communicating like mud." Emmett waited until he heard the front door slam, then sat up, fully clothed and full of vigor. "Blundering kid." He swung his legs off the bed like a man half his age and scrambled around the apartment, to the phone to call a cab, to the full-length mirror to smooth any wrinkles in his sweater and trousers. In all his haste he almost forgot the two keys to everything. That wouldn't do. Wouldn't do at all!

RON RETURNED to the apartment hours later, beet-red and seething. He stalked up to Emmett, who was calmly seated in his *Death of a Salesman* rocker, reading a book.

"You knew it was going to happen! Knew!"

Emmett carefully slipped a bookmark between the pages he was reading. "What are you going on about?"

"Santa Claus! You knew I'd have to take your place at the Pole."

"Really!" Emmett savored the image. "How'd you do?"

His interest threw Ron off balance. He sank down on the arm of his grandfather's chair. "I don't know. Nobody threw tomatoes."

"Splendid. Thanks so much."

"You knew, though, Pop. That was a dirty trick."

"Stanley Bickel's cousin is standing by—"

"Not anymore," Ron cut in rudely. "He's in jail on some kind of traffic offense."

Emmett raised his eyes. "Oh, my stars."

"Lenora admitted that the whole store knows about it."

Emmett's chest heaved. "Very well. I did know about the bad-seed Bickel. But I really couldn't go in today, and my contract makes me responsible for the position—"

"Bickel explained all of that as he threw the suit on me."

"Well, in any case, I'll be more than happy to return on the morrow."

Ron exhaled. "No, you're fired."

"Fired!"

"Sacked, terminated, history. Bickel insisted. Said if we caused trouble he would sue."

Emmett made a cackling sound. "Oh well, just let him try to find a replacement, with two more shopping days till Christmas."

Ron released another breath, and patted the old man's shoulder. "He won't have to. It's me. For the duration."

"You! Ronny!"

"I'm sorry, Pop. But it's the only terms he'd agree to. He said the line moved quicker, and Lenora's production at the service desk was way up."

"Oh, I see." Emmett bit his lip thoughtfully.

"Are you mad?" Ron asked in concern.

"No, I understand you were trapped. And I had a long and satisfying run up there at the Pole." He smiled broadly then. "Told you you had what it takes to shine in the footlights. It'll be kind of nice, having glossy photos of each of us in action. Santa and son." He gestured to the wall behind the television. "I'll hang them both there."

Ron's eyes crinkled at the corners. "Yeah, sure. A couple of mad troopers."

Emmett beamed approvingly. "Even though you're my grandson, you've always been just like a son to me. The son I never had."

"I know, Pop. Just the way..."

"The way what?"

"Never mind." Ron left the room quickly as his eyes moistened. He'd so foolishly begun to view Toby as the son he'd never had. Ron and Toby, father and son. The idea that Jeanne could just cut him off, because she'd been influenced by her parents' anger and their doubts, split his heart in two.

13

JEANNE'S PHONE RANG early on Christmas Eve morning. Just after six. Thinking it was the alarm on her clock radio, she gave the snooze button several vicious stabs with her index finger. When that didn't work, she felt her way across the nightstand to her telephone, snagged the receiver and drew it down into her warm cocoon.

"Merry, Merry Christmas," she mumbled into the mouthpiece.

"This is Elaine, Jeanne. Elaine Rosetti."

"Oh, Elaine." Jeanne blinked rapidly and struggled to sit up. Damn that Ron. Had he told his pals their problems?

"Just called to say that of course we get the *Clarion* delivered to our doorstep here in Minneapolis—"

"I don't follow you, Elaine."

"Oh, my gosh. I bet it's a surprise from Ron."

"What?" Jeanne knew her voice was sharp, but she couldn't help it. She'd had enough surprises.

"His article."

"Oh, I know about that—"

"The picture of him and Toby is precious. Adorable."

"There's a picture of the two of them?"

"Yes, Ron's putting the red hat on him. Didn't you know?"

"Not about the picture," Jeanne hedged, gathering her groggy wits as quickly as she could. Wasn't that article supposed to be about returning home and recapturing the lost spirit of Christmas or something?

"It's so precious and so revealing," Elaine went on. "I mean, the way it tells about Ron's return, his romance with you, the reawakening of family values inside him." She sniffed. "Oh, gosh, I just started to cry."

"And he named names," Jeanne said incredulously.

"Of course. You're a celebrity!"

Jeanne let her ramble on, and ultimately thanked her again for the wonderful party up north. She just had to see that paper. Right away.

"But where are we goin', Mommy?" Toby whined as Jeanne eased him out of his pajamas and into his clothes.

Jeanne released a harried sigh. "It won't take long. I just have to go buy a newspaper."

"We get one every day. On the step. I'll show you, Mommy."

"No, this is a different paper. From Minneapolis."

"Is it better?"

"Your picture's in there. With Ron."

"Me and Ronny!" His hazel eyes grew. "Gravy dam!"

The front bell rang just as she was helping Toby with his boots. She whisked open the door to find Emmett standing on the other side in a black felt hat and topcoat, a stack of papers in his arms.

"Wouldn't dare kill the messenger, would you?"

She grinned wryly. "Not on Christmas, Emmett. Please, come in."

Toby took the papers, raced into the living room, and plopped down on the floor. Jeanne went to retrieve one copy and guided Emmett back to the kitchen. "I'm afraid all I have to drink is grape juice," she announced. "Haven't had time to make coffee."

Emmett set his hat on the table. "Then grape juice it shall it be. Never had it before, but I'm game."

Jeanne brought a small glass to the table, her fingers itching to get hold of the paper.

"I feel there's something I should explain first," Emmett began.

"Elaine Rosetti already called with the details," she informed him. "As did several Potter relatives once removed. And an old grade-school teacher who never liked my handwriting. I know full well that Ron wrote about me, about us."

"Well, I just couldn't help feeling that you didn't have enough faith in Ron's sentiments."

"You felt? What do you mean, Emmett?"

"I'm here, because again I'm responsible for this situation." The old man studied his veined hands. "This article, as it stands, isn't as Ron meant it to be. It includes excerpts from his private journal."

With a horrified gasp, Jeanne fumbled with the paper.

"He submitted a much more superficial version to Burt Waters, the editor. I later delivered the second, more personal, disk, as well as the photo to Burt, claiming that Ron wanted him to blend it all together if he could."

"Ron must be ready to kill you!"

Emmett cleared his throat, fumbling with his tie. "No, I don't think so..."

"No?"

"He's still sleeping at the moment and hasn't a clue. I unplugged the telephone and closed his door."

She regarded him in exasperation. "Oh, Emmett."

"Thought if you spoke to him posthaste, patched things up, he would find the invasion of privacy worth it."

"You are so bad. So very very bad."

"Indeed." He sipped his grape juice docilely. "But I am right, am I not? You backed out because he suddenly was a Potter pariah and perhaps not a sure thing, not worth the fight?"

She hung her head. "Yes, it's true."

He tapped his finger on the paper. "You read this carefully. That's all I ask. If you decide you wish to reach Ron today, he'll be at Grace Brothers all afternoon."

"But why?"

"He's the new Santa there, of course!" He shook his head pityingly. "See what you miss when you slack off for even a day or two?"

She laughed, squeezing his hand. "I guess. Thanks for coming...and everything."

He drained his juice and stood up. "Oh, by the way, I must say I think you Potters owe me an apology."

Her forehead furrowed. "Now Emmett..."

"Well, it's partly my fault for refusing to have a look at your boy in the first place."

"What are you driving at?"

"Well, I didn't think I could recall his wishes. And understandably, because I did see hundreds upon hundreds of little monkeys."

Elaine thought she'd explode. "Emmett! The point. What is it?"

"I do remember Toby quite clearly. Not because of the toys he wanted, naturally. Not because of your lovely mother. But because of his last wish, so surprising, so delightful, so...splendid."

Jeanne peeled off her blue parka, joyously listening to Emmett's explanation. "Say, would you like another glass of grape juice?"

He nodded. "I believe I would. Good stuff, isn't it?"

GRACIE'S CURRENT SANTA couldn't help stealing a look at his watch that afternoon around two-fifty. Christmas Eve traffic in the store was thinning. Closing was scheduled for three.

It had been a slow day at the North Pole. Which was not surprising as it was a little late for the red man to make dreams come true. Or to have his own realized, for that matter.

How ironic that Jeanne should show up in the final minutes, wearing the same kind of determined expression she'd worn the first time they met in this place.

This time he watched her approach in her light blue jacket from behind his snowy white beard. His heart thundered in his chest, causing an alarming ringing in his ears. What could she possibly want now?

Jeanne slowed up near the gingerbread entrance to the Pole. Then, as though propelled by a burst of courage, she moved past the elves and photographer, climbed up the glittery staircase to the throne, and perched herself upon Santa's knee!

Ron cleared his throat. "I'm only the stand-in," he told her in his own personalized St. Nick bellow.

She searched his face frantically. "Don't you think I know who you are?"

"Do you know? Really know?" Ron stared her down with steely control. He was too hurt to assume anything, or to even hope for anything.

"As it happens," she went on, "I've already spoken to your predecessor. It's how I tracked you down."

"I don't understand, Jeanne," he said plaintively. It was sexual agony having her on his knee.

"Emmett came over to the house. With a copy of the article—"

"How did it turn out?"

She gasped in dismay. "Haven't you seen it *yet?*"

"No. Slept in. Came right over here. No one outside of Stanley Bickel and a few others even know who I am or where I am."

"Oh, Ron." She tipped her head against his soft white collar.

"People will talk, Jeanne—"

"You may as well know they're already talking."

"Meaning?"

She lifted her head and fingered his beard. "Don't blow your stack, but Emmett tampered with your article."

Ron's jaw slackened in disbelief. "How? He wouldn't know the first thing about it."

"He took your personal journal disk and the photo of you and Toby to the *Clarion* the other day—"

"Oh, no..."

"It isn't all that bad," she assured him. "It's what made me rush over here."

He lifted a bushy brow. "Yeah?"

"Yeah," she confirmed with a nod. "You were right and I was wrong, Ron. We do belong together. And the depth of your feelings for me and Toby—well, once I saw it in black and white, I melted into mush."

His voice was husky. "Tried to tell you."

"I know. But I was married a long time to a different kind of man. It worked. I was happy. Then you came along and scared me clear to my toenails, Ron. What we shared was so sudden and intense, so—so different."

"Maybe I just seemed too damn good to be true," he teased.

Her eyes twinkled. "Gravy dam, you did."

He asked cautiously, "How about that family of yours? Is there a hangman's noose waiting?"

"No, not at all," she said happily. "Why, once I called the Potters over to my place for an emergency meeting with Emmett—"

"You did what!"

Her blue eyes grew misty. "Oh, Ron." She sniffed. "Emmett did remember Toby once he saw him."

"You're joking!"

"No. And do you know why?"

"Can't begin to guess."

Her lower lip trembled. "Because he wanted a new man around the house. Our house! Apparently he was tired of playing my little soldier—and baseball—all by himself."

"Then Emmett was right, wasn't he?" he marveled slowly. "All Toby's dreams are within easy reach."

"If you'll still have us!" Throwing caution to the winds, she gave him a fierce hug.

Ron raised his hand to the redheaded photographer, ready and waiting at the tripod. But she didn't need the cue. The moment Jeanne pressed her lips to his, the bulb flashed. Why, anyone could plainly see the shot was picture-perfect.